"Eight weeks alone is a long time."

Jassim flung her a look through the shadows as he continued. "Especially when your only commitment is to play a harp twice nightly. I seem to remember a quote on the lines of Satan finding mischief for idle hands to do."

"Just what are you suggesting?" Clemence demanded.

"Don't give me the outraged stare routine," he chided. "There's something fishy about Harrell & Co., and I intend to get to the bottom of it."

Clemence didn't know what to say. How could she fight him? "There's something *I'd* like to get to the bottom of," she countered. "Exactly how much authority do you have at the Al Fori Plaza?"

"None." Jassim replied.

"Then may I suggest you mind your own damn business!" Clemence said as she plunged down the path toward her bungalow.

ELIZABETH OLDFIELD began writing professionally as a teenager after taking a mail-order writing course, of all things. She later married a mining engineer, gave birth to a daughter and a son and happily put her writing career on hold. Her husband's work took them to Singapore for five years, where Elizabeth found romance novels and became hooked on the genre. Now she's a full-time writer in Scotland and has the best of both worlds—a rich family life and a career that fits the needs of her husband and children.

Books by Elizabeth Oldfield

Don't miss any of our special offers. Write to us at the following address for information on our newest releases.

Harlequin Reader Service
901 Fuhrmann Blvd., P.O. Box 1397, Buffalo, NY 14240
Canadian address: P.O. Box 603,
Fort Erie, Ont. L2A 5X3

ELIZABETH OLDFIELD

quicksands

Harlequin Books

TORONTO • NEW YORK • LONDON
AMSTERDAM • PARIS • SYDNEY • HAMBURG
STOCKHOLM • ATHENS • TOKYO • MILAN

Harlequin Presents first edition May 1988
ISBN 0-373-11077-4

Original hardcover edition published in 1987
by Mills & Boon Limited

CHAPTER ONE

CLEMENCE felt a curious *frisson*. The man had arrived. Eyes downcast as her fingers skipped and twirled across the strings of her harp, she had not seen him enter the hotel lobby, yet she *knew*. Some sixth sense had warned her. She sneaked a look across to the corner he habitually staked out as his own. Yes, there he was. Tall and powerfully built, he had eased the battered slouch hat back from his brow to stand with arms folded, studying her. Hurriedly she withdrew her gaze. Who was he? When she had first noticed him days ago, her reaction had been flippant. The hat, allied with the khaki short-sleeved shirt and trousers he wore, made him a dead ringer for the screen hero Indiana Jones. Since then her assessment had changed. Now 'white hunter' seemed a more appropriate definition, because increasingly Clemence felt she was being stalked. Yet it was not as though the man admired her and had capture for his own private zoo in mind. On the contrary, his presence lay more on the lines of her being a dangerous—even rabid— animal which, at all costs, must be held at bay.

In the pause which separated a hop-along folk tune from the start of a medley, Clemence shot him another swift glance. The bedraggled state of his clothes indicated that the 'white hunter' was, more mundanely, a workman. The sultry complexion and strands of black hair which tumbled on to his brow specified a local Omani workman. But in that case, shouldn't he be wearing robes and a turban? Also, Arab males invariably sport a moustache and a beard, yet he possessed neither. Not that he was clean-shaven—dark

5

growth gave evidence that several days had elapsed since
his chin had come into contact with a razor. He looked
scruffy, in a rakish kind of way. Recalling the trend which
had actors and pop stars neglecting to shave in order to
nurture what had been styled 'designer stubble', Clemence
gave a wry, inward laugh. She could not imagine this
character concerning himself with such narcissistic man-
oeuvres. His brawniness came courtesy of nature, not by
contrivance with his mirror. Yet rough and tough though
his appearance was, he possessed an aura of . . . sophistication. A sophistication which jarred with the humble
workman image, as his appearance amongst the well-
dressed hotel guests also jarred. Regular as clockwork, he
had put in an appearance at six p.m. on Monday, Tuesday,
Wednesday—Clemence frowned, realising he had
marched in to monitor her performance every single
evening since Howard's departure. Had he been around
before then? She did not think so.

Others listened to her music: the couples who sat on the
yolk-yellow leather sofas, the businessmen who lounged
against the balconies which overlooked the marble-pillared
entrance hall: even the begowned Omani engaged in
brewing complimentary coffee over a charcoal burner took
an interest. They didn't threaten. The workman did. He
struck her as being menacingly broody. The Al Fori Plaza
might feature amongst the world's top fifty hotels, be the
ultimate in the Middle East where luxury was concerned,
yet all of a sudden it seemed a totally alien environment
and a very long way from home.

Arms moving with a ballerina's grace, Clemence
recalled her feelings last weekend when the taxi had
whisked Howard off to Seeb Airport in order to catch the
London flight. Annoyance had been uppermost, yet there
was an element of heel-kicking, laughter-making relief. At

times her erstwhile best buddy could be gruesomely pedantic. All that day he had devoted himself to grinding out instructions on what she must do while he was gone.

'Practise your harp each morning. Keep to our usual repertoire. Stay within the hotel grounds and you'll come to no harm.' To prick a protest he saw bubbling, he had amended, 'If you must embark on the odd excursion, make sure Otto goes along, too.'

Clemence had wrinkled her nose. Howard and Otto, the bespectacled Swiss who worked as under-manager, had struck up a firm friendship. She knew why. Because like attracts like. Both young men were pleasant, personable but, it had to be admitted, prone to the kind of *serious* air which goes with dispensing orders.

'Clean your teeth twice a day,' she had sing-songed in return. 'Wash your hands before meals. Don't forget fresh underwear. How old do you think I am—twenty-five or merely five?'

Ignoring her question, Howard had snapped the lock on his suitcase. 'Most importantly, given any admirers the big E. Remember the trouble we had with that gigolo type who tried to attach himself to you in Rome?'

'He was not a gigolo!' she had protested indignantly. 'And OK, he was persistent, but——'

'Besotted,' Howard had grumbled. 'Same as ninety per cent of the guys who clap eyes on you.'

He had been exaggerating. Like any other pretty girl she gathered admirers along the way, but plenty were immune to her charms. The workman, for example! Where did he come from? she wondered. Perhaps he worked on the roads? From the little she had seen of Oman, Clemence knew a massive road-building scheme was in progress, and that would explain his aggressively outdoors air and grimy clothes. Yet it seemed odd that a labourer would possess the

confidence to visit a top-flight hotel in his working gear.
And the man *was* confident. He carried himself with an ease
which declared he accounted to no one.

He could not be a *bona fide* client, Clemence decided as
she started the next tune. To the best of her knowledge, he
never bought a drink nor ate a meal. All he appeared to do
was stride in, check she was in place on the tiny stage which
nestled between the two glass-walled elevators, and stride
out again minutes later. She was surprised the doorman
allowed him entry. If she had been in charge, she would
have challenged his right of admission. Clemence sighed.
No, she wouldn't. Anyone who wished to remain intact
would think twice before blocking the path of such a surly
vagabond.

Howard's warnings, scornfully dismissed, began to
foghorn.

'We both know your knack of attracting the undesirable
element . . . five minutes alone in the desert and you'd be in
the clutches of some cut-throat Beduoin . . . I've read about
tribes in the interior who still trade in slaves, they'd go a
bundle on a petite blonde with hair hanging half-way
down her back.'

At this, Clemence had laughed. 'What do you reckon I'd
fetch on the open market—a brace of camels and a year's
supply of frankincense?'

Beneath the workman's surveillance, laughter no longer
seemed entirely apt. She wished Howard hadn't abandoned
her and shot off to England. Still, he would be back in a
week's time. Or would he? A niggling, wriggling doubt
surfaced. She had few illusions and much as the admission
stung, infuriated, curled her hands into impotent fists, it
could not be denied that Yvonne possessed remarkable pulling power. And even more so in her present
condition. Having drawn him back to her side,

suppose the brunette decided to keep him there? No, she wouldn't, couldn't. Howard had *promised* to return to Oman as scheduled.

The medley finished, Clemence risked a glance. Her censor had gone. Phew! Now she could relax. Tonight's programme featured Country-and-Western, and although the arrangements missed the additional twang of Howard's electric guitar, they still sounded good played on the harp. As she strummed the opening bars of one of her favourite melodies, she smiled. Members of her audience were smiling, too, and tapping fingers and feet. Provide music in a hotel lobby, and often you might as well be both inaudible and invisible, but this evening the response was enthusiastic. A satisfying round of applause greeted her bow half an hour later.

Clemence was involved in sorting out music for her second show in the bar mid-evening, when she noticed Khalid Al Fori walking towards her. Twenty at the most, the young man bore the grand title of 'hotel manager'.

'He's a spoilt rich kid playing at big boss,' Howard had stated. 'Otto reckons his contribution to running this pile is minimal, and that if his daddy hadn't built the Plaza and then obligingly upped and died and left it to him, he'd be sweeping floors.'

Clemence had said nothing. Much as she liked the young Arab—his happy-go-lucky manner reminded her of Pete, her teenage brother—she had had to agree. Every day, around mid-morning, Khalid would descend from the penthouse suite he shared with his mother, and parade around wearing a white, white suit and a white, white smile. He never *did* anything, unless regaling guests with his peculiar brand of fractured English could be classed as an activity.

'Your solo act is top of the pops,' he declared, as she

stepped down from the stage. 'Perhaps you should separate
from your husband for always?' His sable-brown eyes
twinkled. 'And may I compliment you on the—what is
it?—cattle-girl outfit.'

'Cowgirl,' she corrected, grinning. As added glitz for
their act she and Howard wore eye-catching clothes, and to
match the night's music she was decked out in a fringed
buckskin waistcoat and pants, teamed with pale leather
boots and a stetson. Clemence's grin faded. 'You don't think
my appearance might be regarded as too——'

'Raunchy?' inserted Khalid, chuckling like an impudent
schoolboy.

'Well, yes,' she agreed, surprised his vocabulary
stretched that far. 'Women do dress more conservatively in
the Middle East, and I've no wish to offend.'

'You are performing within a cosmopolitan hotel before
a cosmopolitan clientele,' he pointed out. 'But even if you
were playing your harp in the streets, who is going to take
offence at a beautiful young lady with a handspan waist
and such deliciously long legs?'

Clemence gave a wry look. Straight facts would have
been preferable to floweriness, but she baulked at pushing
for a clearer ruling on the dress code. Khalid's English
could be erratic, his accent chocolatey. When speaking
with him she needed to concentrate, and even then odd
phrases escaped her. Yet despite these dead spots in
communication, she enjoyed his company. A fully-fledged
local, he was able to provide an insight into the mysterious
land of Oman. From the start he had generously answered
her many questions. He had been generous in other ways,
too.

She glanced at the board, set to one side of the stage, which
continued to announce *Harrell & Co.—Musical Duo*.

'Thanks again for agreeing to my appearing alone.'

'No bother.' Khalid smoothed olive-skinned fingers over a trim black beard, his pride and joy. 'I consider your husband should be commended for his desire to be at his mother's bedside during her last days.'

Clemence dredged up a weak smile. Commended? At his mother's bedside? Oh dear, if only the young man knew the truth! Deceptions, minor or major, always disturbed her, yet what option did she have but to go along with the story Howard had concocted? Revealing the true motivation for his hasty departure would have been impossible. Admittedly social mores were lackadaisical these days, but never so lackadaisical that he could request permission to visit a pregnant girl-friend, while leaving his wife behind!

Khalid touched her elbow.

'You'll join me for a drink,' he said, and without waiting for a reply, led her forward.

The bar, a low-ceilinged den decorated in uniform shades of clay and beige, made a popular rendezvous later in the evening, but currently its occupants comprised a bored waiter and a trio of Japanese businessmen grouped around a far table. Snapping to life, the waiter smiled as they perched themselves on tall chrome and suede bar-stools, then brandished the cocktail list and made energetic suggestions. The speciality of the week was, he explained, a bacchanalian mix of Campari, vodka, Korean ginseng and five other weird and wonderful ingredients. When they settled for a simple lime juice each, it did nothing for his day.

'The last time we spoke, you told me about some of the old customs,' prompted Clemence, intent on steering the conversation clear of further references to her mother-in-law's state of health. She removed her stetson and dropped it down against the foot of her stool, then bounced life back into her rich, corn-coloured mane with her fingers. 'You promised to tell me more.'

A girl with a zest for experiences, for travel, Clemence could never hear enough about how the rest of the world functioned. She found it endlessly fascinating. Yet even better than listening would have been seeing for herself. A look at the sky, one sniff at the breeze, and she was raring to go. Go she would have done in Oman, if Howard had not resisted. But he had clung like a limpet to the hotel, within easy reach of a telephone and the pesky Yvonne.

'Until the early nineteen-seventies,' Khalid began, 'when the cannons of Fort Mirani were fired at sunset, the great doors in Muscat's boundary walls would be bolted. Thereafter any person walking the streets was required by law to carry an oil lamp.' He beamed, delighted because the girl beside him was soaking up his words like a sponge. 'Another law forbade the wearing of sunglasses.'

Clemence laughed. 'No sunglasses? Why ever not?'

'Because it's too easy to hide behind them?' a low voice suggested. 'There's nothing to beat eyeball-to-eyeball contact. You can learn so much that way, can't you, Mrs Harrell?'

Her head whipped round. She had not heard anyone approach and now she nearly toppled off her stool in surprise. The words had come from the workman. He stood little more than a yard away, looking as disreputable as ever.

'Er—yes,' she got out, aware Khalid was also having difficulty with his balance.

'Jass, what are you doing here?' he asked, scrambling to extract his heels from the chrome scaffolding. 'I thought——'

'You thought I'd gone home, and while the cat's away the mice, etcetera, etcetera?'

Presumably the words were meant for Khalid, yet the

man's gaze centred on Clemence. In bare feet she would not have reached much beyond his shoulder, but hoisted on a stool she found herself dead level with his ocean-green eyes. They were deep-set and lustrous, the kind of eyes you could die for. But an Arab with green eyes? An Arab workman who spoke such flawless English? He did have an accent, yet it was very different from Khalid's.

'You're Australian!' she exclaimed.

'You're anti-Oz?' he thrust back.

'No, no. I'm just—I had no idea,' she bumbled, flashing a smile which was meant to apologise for what must have sounded like an accusation.

Beside her, Khalid had managed to recover his poise. 'May I introduce my half-brother, Jassim?' he said.

She stuck out her hand. 'Good evening.'

Working on the basis that a devil you know is better than one you don't, Clemence was grateful for this chance to meet him. He was another Al Fori? Life brimmed with surprises. She would never have guessed a relationship, yet having been alerted could detect likenesses. The colour of the eyes might be different, yet each brother was endowed with the same hedging of luxuriant, black lashes. Their noses, fine-chiselled and slightly hawked, were similar too. Hazarding a guess that the newcomer must be in his early thirties, it seemed possible that ten years ago he might also have been an attractive cherub, a handsome boy. However, time and experience had honed the boy into a man. The rounded contours had disappeared, leaving him lean-faced and stern-jawed. His skin was paler than his brother's, not as swarthy, and seen in close-up his dark hair contained glints of chestnut brown. He looked less Arab, more European. Another difference—*the* difference—was that in contrast to Khalid's affable indolence, the older man exuded a sense of under-skin energy which she found both

compelling and dangerous. Given the correct stimulus,
Jassim Al Fori would generate sufficient electricity to light
up entire towns. He was not someone to be ignored. As if
Clemence did not know that already!

'Good evening,' he replied.

His handclasp was firm and concise, his smile merely
concise. As she realised these motions of civility were
nothing but motions, Clemence's temper began to ripple.
The expressive register of his green eyes indicated, without
a shadow of doubt, that he disapproved of her even more at
close range than from a distance. Yet on what grounds did
she merit his disdain? She had done nothing to upset him,
all she had done was exist. When he continued to weigh her
up and find her wanting, the temper ripples grew into
small waves. Who was he, to subject her to such blatant
criticism? Half-brother, Khalid had said, and much older
at that. Aware that Arab families could be complex
conglomerates of wives and children, Clemence decided the
relationship had to be tenuous. Weren't his clothes clear
evidence that he moved in entirely different cirles from the
debonair Khalid? Jassim's branch of the family must have
fallen from grace, if indeed it had ever been in grace, or else
why wasn't he involved in the running of the Al Fori
Plaza? Having convinced herself he was small fry, she felt
sturdier.

'Would you like a drink, Jass?' Khalid enquired.

'No, thanks. I only came back because I'd forgotten to
make a phone call.' Legs set apart, thumbs hung in the slit
pockets of his worn trousers, he surveyed Clemence. 'I
presume your husband left written permission for you to
fraternise with gentlemen in bars?'

At a pinch the question could be construed as humorous;
the tone was not. She bristled, knowing full well Jassim Al
Fori was accusing her of hobnobbing with his baby brother

while Howard was safely out of the way.

'If you've checked your calendar recently you'll recall we are in the twentieth century. Which means,' she informed him coolly, 'married women get to make their own decisions.'

'Yes?'

'Yes. And I personally don't require anyone's permission to do anything.'

'You don't love, honour and obey?' he drawled.

Clemence frowned. 'I didn't say that.'

'Didn't you?'

True enough, eyeball-to-eyeball contact could not be beaten. The sea-green eyes condemned her outright.

'Does it matter if I'm not kept under lock and key twenty-four hours a day?' she enquired, giving a smile, a glassy one, to show she refused to be intimidated.

'It matters.' His voice was quiet, but nuances rang out loud and clear. 'Don't forget, you're in the Sultanate of Oman, Mrs Harrell.'

'And if you weren't Mrs Harrell, you wouldn't be,' Khalid piped up. The youth had been following the conversation with varying degrees of comprehension, but now it was Clemence who was lost.

'I beg your pardon?'

'The entry of single Western women into Oman is restricted,' Jassim told her, by way of translation. 'Don't look so shocked. There's a good reason for the control, and there are exceptions.'

'Such as?' she demanded.

'Girls whose fathers work here are allowed to visit, and I believe permission's granted for those in certain job categories.'

'Jobs like mine?' Clemence suggested.

His laugh was insulting. 'No way, sunshine. Vital jobs

like doctors, lecturers, and other highly trained personnel. They're welcome, but otherwise the door's closed to unmarried Western women.'

'Why?' she asked in bewilderment.

Khalid grinned. 'The authorities don't want us to be overrun by bar girls and——' He turned to his brother.

'Hookers,' Jassim provided. Once again the muscular arms were folded across his chest, and he was subjecting her to an intense scrutiny. 'Plus any other kind of female whose aim it is to get her claws on some Arab cash.'

'You're kidding!'

'I'm not.' He wasn't. He was deadly serious.

'Gold-diggers are a tiny percentage,' Clemence protested.

'Maybe, yet one rotten apple can spoil an entire box. Don't forget this is, for the most part, a primitive country. Only for the past sixteen or seventeen years has Oman acknowledged the twentieth century. Now, by treading carefully, the hope is to embrace what's good in the developed world, and avoid the bad. Which means refusing entry to riff-raff.'

Khalid summed up. 'So if you weren't Mrs Harrell, you wouldn't be here.'

'That can't be right,' she started to say, but Jassim intervened. Fortunately, Clemence realised seconds later for if she had completed her statement she could have landed herself in all kinds of trouble. From now on, she must engage brain before operating mouth.

'The impact of the outside world's controlled by prohibiting the fly-by-night element,' he continued, ramming his point home. 'Every visitor must be sponsored, as the hotel sponsored you and your husband. Which means, Mrs Harrell, you're under an obligation to behave yourself.'

'I *am* behaving myself.'

'Keep it that way.'

He was using that quiet, nuance-filled voice again, a voice which made her blue-grey eyes blaze. Ye gods, what kind of a woman did he imagine he was talking to? In the midst of preparing an acid reply, Clemence's attention was diverted and she flung out a tempestuous hand.

'Would you kindly get off my stetson? You happen to be standing on it. See?' When Jassim stepped back and bent to retrieve the leather hat, she grabbed it from him as though it was her first-born which he had kidnapped. 'Have you any idea how much these things cost?' she demanded, robustly channelling her dislike of him and his insinuations into this misdemeanour. Clemence glared fit to kill. 'My stetson's a darn sight too valuable to be used as a doormat!'

'Forgive me.'

The apology was sincere, but brief. Too brief. She would have much preferred him to grovel, though grovelling was not Jassim Al Fori's style. Indeed, she had a nasty suspicion he found her outrage comical. The hint of amusement which lurked around his eyes fanned her temper. Clemence did not appreciate being laughed at by a man who, minutes ago, had been close to accusing her of adultery and worse! She frowned down, searching for a dent in the brim, a scratch, something which would justify her indignation. She found nothing.

'I'll buy you a new hat,' Khalid offered.

'Thanks, but——' She turned to him, a smile at the ready to accompany her firm refusal, but Jassim was there first.

'Oh no, you won't,' he growled. From being amused, the green eyes had become icy emeralds. He thrust off the slouch hat to rake a hand through his tangled mass of dark hair. 'Don't you dare become involved. Do you have a death wish or something?'

Involved? Death wish? The man talked in riddles.

'Slow down,' pleaded Khalid. 'When you shoot out words like bullets from a machine gun, I can't understand.'

'Learn from experience.' The grated reply gave way to a hiss of frustration. 'Skip it, I'll explain later, but for now just you do as I tell you, and——'

'My stetson's fine,' Clemence interrupted. Jassim's stance disturbed her. Clearly, he ate too much red meat. He was scowling at his brother as though if he didn't grasp the point he would *make* him understand, perhaps by means of a swift rearrangement of the boy's jawbone. The desire to end this family in-fighting had her jamming the stetson on her head and circulating a toothpaste smile. 'No need for a replacement.' she chirruped.

Jassim swung round and, in reflex, her heart missed a beat. His irritation had been such that she would not have been surprised if he had grabbed her by the lapels of her waistcoat and shaken her until the stetson fell off, but whatever it was which had incensed him, the moment had passed.

'Fine, that's settled. If your hat suffers a relapse, please let me know,' he instructed, switching on a charm she would not have believed possible if she had not seen for herself how his lips curved, how the green eyes crinkled, how a long vertical dimple split one cheek. Clemence needed to fight against being dazzled. As a charmer you're not bad, she assessed. In fact, he was formidably good. 'Should a period in intensive care be required, I'm more than willing to offer you the services of this——' an index finger flicked at the brim of the slouch hat held in his hand, '—while yours is indisposed. That is, if you're desperate for headgear.'

Disarmed by the full blast of his smile, Clemence was about to respond in kind when she remembered how, for the past six days, he had marched into the hotel and ruthlessly monitored her. This was not charm, this was manipulation.

'I'll never be that desperate,' she retaliated, crisp as crackers. 'Though if I were, I'd know where to contact you, wouldn't I? You do seem to be my most ardent fan. I'd feel utterly forlorn without you in my audience.'

He replaced his hat, and looked steadily at her from beneath the brim.

'Then in your audience I'd better remain, hadn't I? Which suits me fine because, Mrs Harrell, that was my intention from the start.'

So much for a vote of confidence! she thought, as he turned on his heel and walked away. Jassim Al Fori's hostility was a potent force. Yet it seemed others in Oman, namely the authorities, might also be hostile if one pertinent fact ever came to light. Clemence raised her glass of lime and took a long, deep swallow. She and Howard might have gone as far as to share a bungalow in the hotel grounds and call themselves man and wife, but they had never gone as far as the altar. How would the powers-that-be react to that?

CHAPTER TWO

MORE at ease now his brother had departed, Khalid returned to relating local customs, yet although Clemence made a pretence of listening her thoughts were thousands of miles away—with Howard. Throughout their four-year liaison, her partner had dealt with the paperwork engendered in touring the international hotel circuit and so had completed the forms necessary for visas and such which had allowed them entry into Oman. How had he classified her? she wondered. The pretence of being his wife was one she accepted on a superficial, verbal level, but his making a counterfeit declaration in black and white was different.

Clemence finished her drink. She itched to escape, but with the young Arab in full swing a quick exit was not easy. She waited a while, then, as he paused for breath and her patience ran out, gabbled rapid excuses and departed. On speedy legs, she powered across the palatial entrance hall, out on to the flagstoned terrace, and down the steps into the gardens. She needed to speak to Howard, needed her position clarified. Could she be in the country under false pretences—and thus liable to being slung out on her neck at any moment—or had perhaps a special dispensation been granted because she had come here as part of a double act?

Nearing the Andalusian-style guest bungalow, Clemence nipped her lower lip between her teeth and frowned. Before he had left, one of Howard's most repeated commands had been 'Don't ring me, I'll ring you'. Long-distance telephone calls were costly, even more so through a hotel switchboard. Once the outlay would not have

bothered him—the big, blond guitarist had had a generous
approach towards spending, hence their quality stage
outfits—but the prospect of parenthood had wrought a
dramatic change. Overnight he had become a miser. What
could be saved, must be saved. Every penny counted.
Which, she thought derisively, doubtless accounted for a
week having gone by without his reporting back on what
was happening at home. On the other hand, it could more
brutally be a case of her being out of sight, out of mind
because Yvonne, and only Yvonne, mattered to Howard
now. His devotion left everyone else out in the cold, and
heigh-ho to any closeness they had shared in the past!

Clemence unlocked the door, tossed her stetson on to the
settee, and grabbed up the telephone. Forget penny-
pinching, this was an emergency. A month prior to their
coming to Oman, and disregarding her pithily voiced
objections, Howard had moved into the brunette's flat, and
this was the number she asked for now.

'No answer,' the hotel telephonist reported cheerfully,
when the ringing tone sounded on and on and on. 'Would
you like me to try later?'

'Please.'

With a sigh, Clemence replaced the receiver. Time
difference made it mid-afternoon in the UK, which meant
Howard and his lover could be anywhere—strolling hand
in hand by the river, loading up a supermarket trolley, or
. . . at the hospital? The last option produced a silent groan.
At the time of her tearful summons, Yvonne had been vague.
There had been twinges. She did not feel 'right'. Female
intuition warned that something was amiss. Considering
she had not even contacted the local surgery, Clemence had
been amazed when Howard had treated the call as a
Mayday signal and promptly upped sticks. *Her* intuition
said 'poor little me' was involved in emotional theatricals,
as usual. Yuck! Also she had not been immune to the fact

that the request for Howard's presence could be interpreted as a move in a power game. What better way for Yvonne to demonstrate supremacy than to crook a finger and sit smugly tight? Clemence dumped herself down on the sofa and tugged off a boot. Howard's reaction left no doubt as to who scored all the sixes now.

But perhaps she was being unkind and Yvonne's fears *did* have substance. Deciding to reserve judgement, she attempted to make contact half an hour later, but failed. She tried again both before and after her evening performance; no luck then, either. Incommunicado and disgruntled, she went to bed.

There was still no reply when the operator dialled the number the next morning. Stretched out on a lounger beside the palm-tree-shaded pool, Clemence wavered between two scenarios. Either Yvonne's cry for help derived from a genuine danger of her losing the baby; in which case she sympathised. Or the brunette had been indulging herself and on Howard's arrival—surprise, surprise—had made a miraculous recovery. Past experience had her veering towards the latter scene, which meant the two of them could well be living it up somewhere. Yvonne's interests ranged from dining out in the nearby Hampshire countryside, to London shopping and theatre trips, to popping over to France for long weekends.

Turning the page on her doorstop-sized paperback, Clemence looked up as a shadow fell over her. It was Otto, business-suited, straight-backed and smiling gratuitously.

'Enjoying the sunshine?' he enquired.

'If you'd asked me that a month ago, I'd have said yes. Now——' She pulled a face. Sunbathing for weeks on end is boring, boring, boring! Claustrophobia's beginning to set in. If this hotel were in a town, I could have browsed around the *souks*, visited a mosque or two, but it isn't. It's in the middle of nowhere. OK, there's that tiny fishing village at the far end of the beach, but I'm fed up with going along to look at the same four boats.'

'The Plaza's convenient for the airport and central to most of the major industrial sites,' the Swiss quoted, sounding like the brochure in her room.

'Agreed, but to get anywhere half-way interesting you need to take a taxi or hire a car, and travel miles.'

'You'd be ill-advised to travel miles on your own. Howard told me how much you'd enjoyed going out and about when the pair of you worked in various European capitals, but this is the Middle East and very different.'

She spread her hands. 'Which is precisely why I want to explore, absorb the atmosphere.'

'It's difficult for a woman to do that on her own. Tourism has yet to take off here. Guided tours and trips around the bay don't exist.' Otto adjusted his spectacles. 'I'm not free until Thursday, but perhaps you would allow me to show you some of the sights then?'

Clemence smiled. 'Sounds like a good idea.'

I must be getting desperate, she thought, as the under-manager returned to his duties. A week ago she had had no intention of going anywhere with Otto—thank you, Howard darling!—but her boredom had consolidated until now she was prepared to grab the chance of any action. Well, not *any* action. She continued to field off the middle-aged business executives and vacationing oil men who had an eye for an unaccompanied blonde. Ritual flirting held no appeal. What excited her was the thought of the Arab country which lay, so near and yet so far, at the end of the drive. Clemence slid a shoestring strap from one shoulder and reached for the coconut oil. Thursday was four days away. In four days' time she would be out there, and never mind if it was with Otto. There seemed little point hanging on until Howard returned, because he might well refuse to budge from the hotel grounds yet again.

She was happily musing over the prospect of a modicum of freedom, when her happiness hiccuped. Would that freedom, that change of scene, release her from thinking about Jassim Al Fori? She hoped so, for interlaced with the confusion over her status in Oman had been confusion about his attitude towards her. She obviously represented some kind of *bête noire*, but why? Already she had spent far too much time toying with possibilities, yet could not keep from working through them again. Could he possess an aversion to women or, more specifically, to women in show business? Clemence did not regard herself as a deep-dyed stalwart, like a Hollywood actress or a high-stepping chorus girl, but nevertheless she had experienced distrust from certain quarters.

'You entertain in hotels?' a former schoolmistress had gasped on meeting her, using tones which equated her harp-playing with wrestling nude nightly with a boa constrictor. 'But you were one of my most promising pupils. I always hoped you'd find a niche in the Civil Service!'

And it was not only middle-aged spinsters who viewed her career as not quite respectable; younger friends had indicated doubts by luridly questioning her about the casting-couch syndrome. Even her parents, both working musicians themselves, had been reluctant about their only daughter becoming involved in what they had termed 'razzamatazz'. If she had been an anonymous harpist in an orchestra—fine. But to be publicised as the female half of Harrell & Co—they were dubious.

'Everyone'll forget about the music and ogle you,' her father had declared.

'Dad, the money's far more than I'd ever make playing in concert halls,' she had protested. 'And as a bonus there's all that wonderful travel.'

'Will you be safe?' her mother had fretted.

'Of *course*. I'm a big girl now. Besides, Howard'll be around to chaperon.'

Her father had pressed a wad of tobacco into his pipe, sighed, and then admitted reluctantly, 'Yes, I dare say he'll keep an eye on you.'

Clemence sat up to knot a zebra-print kanga over her bikini. Howard was not keeping his eye on her now, though doubtless Jassim Al Fori would arrive at six o'clock to give her a visual frisking over. Why was she on his blacklist? Maybe he didn't like blondes? Maybe he had a phobia about harps? Maybe ...

That evening, she climbed on stage barnacled with anticipation. Grow up, she told herself. All Jassim will do, can possibly do, is stand and glower. Ignore him. Any problem is his, not yours. Dance music was the programme theme, and the dress she wore, a long-skirted, flounced extravaganza in white with red polka-dots, owed its inspiration to a mating of flamenco and waltz. Ideally her mood should have combined the *olé* with the lyrical, but all Clemence felt was edgy. If she could have spoken to Howard it would have helped, yet throughout the day one call after another had gone unanswered.

The first half of her session was spent waiting for Jassim to arrive, and when his corner remained stubbornly vacant, she then spent the second half wondering *if* he was going to arrive. If was much worse. In the event, he did not show up. Alleluia, Clemence thought, wringing herself out afterwards like a wet rag. His close-quarters inspection must have provoked a reassessment. He had come to his senses and realised she was not equipped with horns and a tail.

Taking her place in the bar for the second show, she

tuned her harp, opened her music, then, just to make
certain, allowed one quick all-seeing glance. The room was
dim, lit by candles flickering inside smoked-glass globes,
but she would have picked out that slouch hat anywhere.
Her Number One Fan had resigned from the club. Thank
goodness!

In the main her audience were European and American
businessmen, with a smattering of Asians and one or two
Omanis in national dress. They received her music well.
She did not have everyone's complete attention, that was
too much to ask in a crowded bar, but there was enough
clapping at her finale to make her efforts worthwhile.
Clemence collected up her sheet music and was slipping it
into a folder when she became aware of a man striding
through the tables. City suit, pale shirt, well brushed dark
hair—subconsciously she assessed him. This would be a
suave company director coming to stun her with a
hackneyed opening gambit. She knew the type of old.
Because these knights in pin-striped armour travelled the
world first class and frequented expensive hotels, they
considered themselves ideal for her bed.

'I trust you weren't too forlorn earlier,' he said, coming to
a halt.

Her eyes grew round. 'It's you!'

'Were you expecting some other guy?' enquired Jassim,
managing to imply that she had queues of men in dirty
raincoats waiting in the wings.

'No, no,' she assured him.

Grime had been sluiced off, the beard growth removed.
He had become *vivid*. Glossy brown-black hair waved to his
collar, there was a sheen to his skin, his eyes seemed an even
deeper shade of that amazing green. She noted the elegant
line of his charcoal-grey suit, saw his shirt was a classic
snowy-white. Gold cuff-linked cuffs fell over strong, tanned

hands with square-cut and noticeably clean fingernails.
Fascinated by this swap from sweat-stained labourer to
man-about-town, Clemence stood and gaped.

'What's the latest on your mother-in-law?' he asked.

It took a moment to summon up an answer. 'Oh, she's—
she's fine.'

'Strange, I understood her to be knocking at death's
door.'

Her cheeks burned and Clemence was grateful for the
gloom. 'She is. I meant—I meant she's not in any pain. She's
as well as can be expected.'

'That's a relief.'

'Yes.'

She gathered up her folder, gave a curt nod to denote
dismissal, then set off towards the exit. All too soon she
discovered him walking beside her. Jassim was not ready to
be dismissed. Had she really thought he would be?

'Your husband's determination to be with his mother
borders on the——' he split the sentence in such a way her
stomach plunged, '—obsessive. I happened to be in
Khalid's office when he presented his case for going home,
and he sounded——' another chilling split, '—frantic.'

'He was. He is,' Clemence agreed, thinking furiously.

She had not been aware that Jassim had sat in on the
meeting. Why hadn't Howard told her? And if someone
had had to be present, why must it be a man as leery as the
one who was prowling beside her across the lobby like an
untethered panther?

'Something's been puzzling me,' he continued, making
her stomach plunge again. 'I can't understand how, after
what sounds to have been a chequered history of heart
problems, the doctors can pinpoint your mother-in-law's
demise so accurately. Could you explain?'

'She's fading fast,' waffled Clemence.

He threw her a glance. 'I hope she doesn't change her mind.'

'Meaning?'

'Just that your husband's allowed her fourteen days maximum, not a second more, to kick the bucket, as we vulgar Colonials say.'

Her fingers tightened on the music folder. Was this pretend mother-in-law supposed to have suffered a heart attack, an unsuccessful operation, or what? Cardiac trouble, Howard had blithely told her, but too late she saw she should have asked him to repeat his conversation with Khalid word by word. As accomplices went they had an extremely flimsy story, but then they had never reckoned on the FBI arriving in the form of Jassim Al Fori.

'Do you work on the roads?' Clemence asked brightly.

'At times. I'm involved with ready-mixed concrete. Suppose the old gal refuses to comply with the timetable?' he queried, showing a stout disinclination to let go of the subject. 'Suppose she lingers? What happens then? Does your husband return next weekend, as promised?'

'He does.'

'You sound very definite.'

'I am.' Clemence undertook a mental crossing of her fingers.

'You must admit there's a chance it might not work out quite that way.'

She was not prepared to admit anything, and as Jassim held open the swing door which led to the terrace, she sped out ahead of him. Spotlights in scarlet, flame and white shone among the garden foliage, picking out a tumble of blossoms here, fronds of a palm-tree there. Fairyland had been created, but Clemence was blind to any magic. All her energy was concentrated on eluding the trap he seemed determined to spring. Khalid might have taken her partner's excuse for going home at face value, Jassim had not.

'Let's work on the assumption that your husband continues to be absent,' he said, walking with her down the shallow steps to skirt the pool area. 'The pair of you had completed one month of your contract when he decamped, which leaves two to go. It doesn't seem exactly kosher that you should continue receiving the full rate when there's only half a duo on stage, does it?'

'As you were at the meeting, you must know Howard suggested reduced pay,' she replied irritably, 'and that your brother said no.'

'The suggestion was half-hearted, and Khalid has yet to learn the value of a dollar.'

'Look, if Howard doesn't return—though he *will*,' Clemence emphasised, 'I shall insist on receiving only fifty per cent, and retrospective. Happy now?'

'No. Eight weeks alone would be a long time, especially when your only commitment is to play a harp twice nightly.' Jassim paused, then flung her a look through the shadows. 'I seem to remember a quote on the lines of Satan finding mischief for idle hands to do.'

She stopped in her tracks. She had had enough. 'What are you suggesting?' she demanded.

'Don't give me the outraged stare routine, sunshine,' he chided. 'Unlike Khalid, I do possess a certain perceptive skill. There's something fishy about Harrell & Co, and whatever that something is, I intend to get to the bottom of it.'

Clemence did not know what to say. Her instinct was to make a dash for the distant group of red-roofed, white-walled bungalows, and leave her interrogator in the lurch, but that seemed to smack of guilt. Jassim Al Fori had shown himself to be the enemy, so how did she fight him? She searched for a weapon and in recalling his usual appearance, found one. This man spent his days tipping concrete out of a mixer or something similar, that was all.

'There's something *I'd* like to get to the bottom of,' she declared. 'I'd be grateful if you would tell me how much authority you possess with regard to the affairs of the Al Fori Plaza?'

'None.' The eyes which held hers were steady.

'Then may I suggest you allow your brother to worry about the musicians he employs at his hotel?' Clemence said tartly, and plunged on to the path which led to the bungalow. To her consternation Jassim went with her, attaching himself to her side like a Siamese twin. 'In other words, mind your own damn business,' she added, marching along with head held high and gaze pinned straight ahead.

'No way,' he scythed, and his hand came out to catch her upper arm.

'Leave me alone,' she protested, as his fingers bit into her flesh like heated brands. They were marooned amidst a shadowy glade of oleander, with no one else in sight. Clemence felt a surge of fear and ... something else. Without warning she was aware of Jassim as a male, a dominant, sensual male. 'Leave me alone,' she ordered again, furious both with herself and with him. Otto had seemed like acceptable company earlier, but her boredom threshold must be pitifully low if she was going to gaga over some farouche stranger!

'I'll leave you alone if you'll leave Khalid alone,' he retorted, refusing to relinquish his grip.

'Khalid? Me leave Khalid alone?' Since she had turned fifteen, Clemence had been fighting off advances of one sort and another, and now she laughed in his face. Men approached her, not the other way around. 'You think I have designs on your kid brother? You must be joking!'

'I'm not.'

She shook her head in disbelief. 'Be sensible, do I look like the kind of woman who goes on red alert when anything remotely pretty in pants walks by?'

Jassim shrugged. 'Sunshine, you could be a bitch in heat for all I know. And don't forget that in addition to being pretty, Khalid also happens to be impressionable and loaded.'

'Which means I'm going to seduce him?'

'You might try.'

'Try? Try?' Seconds earlier the notion of her pursuing a youth she equated with her teenage brother had seemed comical, but now Clemence was offended. Deeply offended. 'If I did decide to try, I can assure you I'd be successful.'

'Over my dead body,' Jassim snarled softly.

For a moment there was a danger of his intensity swamping her, but the whole situation was too impossible, too unreal, too dramatic. Clemence laughed, her mood changing colour chameleon-like.

'Khalid is——' she hesitated, '—pleasant, but he's a juvenile. OK, maybe in years he's not that much younger than me, but in experience he's——'

'You've been around, then?' Jassim cut in.

'Yes,' she said, only to recognise the question as sneaky a split second later. 'I've been around in so much as I've worked in a lot of different places, met a lot of different people,' she defined.

'I see.'

His voice told her he was seeing all the wrong things.

Clemence sighed. 'You don't honestly imagine Khalid and I have much in common, do you?' she appealed, raising her eyes at the absurdity. 'Besides, how would you suggest two people could conduct a love affair in the middle of a busy hotel?'

'Simple. There are plenty of opportunities if you make them.'

'Like when?'

Jassim's broad shoulders moved. 'Like now.'

A strand of corn-coloured hair was tossed from her shoulder. 'Convince me,' she challenged.

'If you insist,' he said, and before she knew what was happening he pulled her into his arms and kissed her.

The pressure of his mouth was as intoxicating as it was unexpected. His lips took possession of hers, and Clemence skidded through a giddiness to a heady thrill to a feeling of desire. But desiring *him* made no sense at all! The realist inside her skull insisted what was happening must be attributed to biology, to a madcap quirk of chemistry, because being enfolded in his arms felt right. But how could it be right, when it was wrong, wrong, wrong?

'What do you think you're doing?' she demanded, as with breasts heaving and cheeks an indignant pink, she wrenched herself from him.

A dark brow arched. 'Convincing you, Mrs Harrell. Have I been successful?'

'Yes!' Her heart seemed to have broken free from its moorings, and was bobbing up and down in her chest like a boat on a choppy ocean. 'Yes, yes, you have,' she cried. She had not meant it to be a cry, but her voice, like her heart, appeared to be out of control and the words had emerged breathless and squeaky.

'Then I've proved my point,' he said, and strolled away.

Jassim did not hurry, he walked off as calm as a prize fighter who had laid his opponent down on the canvas with a single punch. And poleaxed was how she felt! Bemused, Clemence touched her mouth with the back of her hand, reliving the first brush of his lips. A spin on her heel and she stormed off towards the bungalow. Forget his kiss, it meant nothing. Nothing. She had been kissed before—yet never quite like that. Never with such ... panache.

She wished she hadn't said, 'Convince me.' In retrospect the words sounded provocative, though she had not intended them that way. Or had she? No, playing the flirt was out of character. Clemence had not knowingly meant to goad him, yet from the moment his fingers had closed around her arm she had been aware of sexual attraction. Aware of herself as a woman, soft and yielding. Aware of Jassim as a man, hard and thrusting. What was more, it had been a *mutual* attraction. Like a mosquito, tiny but irritant, it had flown between them. No doubt he would deny it, even to himself, but there had been desire in the sea-green depths of his eyes before he had kissed her. Why had she collaborated? And she had—instinctively—though only for a second. Yet long enough to have ruined her image of herself as someone who spurned casual couplings, and also long enough for her portrayal of the devoted Mrs Harrell to be smashed to smithereens.

Clemence rushed into the bungalow and pounced on the telephone. She was desperate for the balm of a familiar voice. If, yet again, Howard did not answer, then she would ring her own home base. Her parents were presently away on a long-saved-up-for Caribbean cruise, but Pete would be there. Doubtless all the teenager would have to offer would be an up-date on the heavy metal scene and a report of the latest pop concert he had attended, but in her present state of mind even that seemed attractive. Quoting Yvonne's number first, a number which the switchboard operator had to know by heart, she waited. The tone rang and rang then, astonishingly, the telephone was lifted.

'Hello?' said a familiar male voice.

Her mouth spread into a grin. 'Hello, Howard. It's me.'

'Clem? Are you OK?'

Even though their relationship had taken a body-blow of late—maybe not so much a blow as decapitation—just his saying her name made pleasure lap over her. Everything fell into context. She was in a safe and secure environment, alone for just a few more days. This evening a man had kissed her, but it was no cause for alarm, no reason to panic. However much Howard might adopt the role of guardian, hadn't she always been able to take care of herself?

'I'm fine. How are you. How's Yvonne?' Her voice stayed warm. 'I trust the twinges were a false alarm.'

'They were, thank goodness. Why are you phoning me?' he demanded. 'Calls via the Plaza's switchboard cost an arm and a leg, and you know they'll be deducted from our earnings.'

Her pleasure deflated. Once she and Howard had been two people in unison, rarely at odds. Now they spent most of their time conducting a civilised version of guerilla warfare.

'Don't worry, I'll pay for this,' Clemence said tightly. 'I won't deprive you of a a single cent. The reason I'm ringing is to ask how you described me on the forms you filled in before we came to Oman. Was it as a Miss or a Mrs?'

'Mrs. Don't you remember how Bernie reckoned life would be simpler if we went as a married couple?'

'Yes, I do, but——'

'It was no great event. We often say you're my wife.'

'We say it for convenience, not to break the law.' She was snappy. 'And I understood the sham was only as far as the hotel was concerned. I didn't realise you intended to call me Mrs Harrell on official documents.'

'Bernie said disguising a girlfriend or whatever as a wife was common practice to ease entry. He assured me there'd be no repercussions.'

Thinking of their money-mad agent, Clemence snorted.

'Given a chance of making ten per cent, that man would assure you there'd be no repercussions if you laid your head on the block for a re-enactment of the guillotine. It's fine for him to sit in his London office and blithely advocate hoodwinking the authorities, but out here the reality is far less cosy,' she said, and went on to explain what Jassim had told her.

'So we've contravened the rules in a serious way?' Howard mused, when she had finished.

'We have. But what I can't work out is how, if I'm supposed to be married, the single status on my passport wasn't spotted.'

'Clerical blunder—easy done. Look, Clem, you're in Oman, *fait accompli*, so forget the whys and wherefores. If no one knows you're not Mrs Harrell, no one will worry. But for God's sake, keep a low profile. And it'd be wise not to discuss this with anyone. Not even with Otto. The guy's a stickler for doing things properly, and as the hotel's sponsored us and he represents the hotel he might feel it his duty to raise the matter with Customs or whoever. Not to oust you, just for regulation purposes. Working in tandem with me you could be acceptable on a single basis, who knows? But whether you are or not, we can't afford any officials becoming involved. Hell, the British Embassy might be informed you're *persona non grata* and next thing you'll be marched through the airport in handcuffs and thrown on to the first plane.'

'Thank you, Howard. I feel much better now!'

'It'll never come to that,' he soothed hurriedly, 'but don't make waves. Khalid Al Fori's paying us a useful amount of money, so you stick in there, kid. You're doing a great job.'

'How about *you* accompanying me in that great job? When do you plan to arrive next weekend?' There was silence, then she heard him clear his throat—a bad sign.

'Haven't you booked your flight?' Clemence asked.

'Not yet.'

'Howard!'

'The doctor's given Yvonne the all-clear, but——'

'Why you had to be so irresponsible as to get her pregnant in the first place beats me,' she complained.

'She forgot to take her pill.'

'Forgot?' Clemence queried archly.

'Yes, in the heat of the moment it's easily done. Remember how strongly you once felt about that Ralph guy?'

'That was completely different,' she objected. 'You could have had the decency to wait until we'd completed this spell in Oman before you went haywire. It is our final booking.'

'Be charitable!'

Clemence sighed. Charity would have flowed freer if—regardless of how Yvonne had marched in and taken over—she could have understood what Howard saw in the clingy brunette with the cutesy-cutesy voice and cutesy-cutesy appearance. Strewth, what self-respecting female pinned pink satin bows in her hair these days? The only explanation must be that her simpering ways brought out his protective instinct. He was hot on being protective.

'So when can I expect you?' she asked.

'Not for——' He cleared his throat again. 'I'm sure Khalid won't mind if I extend my absence to a month.'

'A month? You intend to be away a whole month?' Clemence squawked in horror. 'Well, Khalid might not mind, but I most certainly would!'

'Your solo act is fine. You need have no fears on that score,' Howard wheedled. 'Weren't you the toast of Düsseldorf when I broke my finger?'

'The musical mechanics don't bother me, reneging on our contract does. Khalid showed no hesitation in letting you go at a moment's notice, but it was on the basis of a firm guarantee that you'd return in a fortnight.'

'Suppose I pare the month down to three and half weeks?'

'That's not much of a concession.'

'I have things to do here.'

'You have things to do in Oman, too,' she reminded him. 'Like keeping faith with our contract.'

'Khalid isn't going to quarrel.'

'I don't care. It isn't good enough'

'But if he's happy, why can't you be?' he pleaded. 'No one likes a pain in the neck, Clem.'

'Then don't be one.'

'A total of less than a month on your own isn't for ever,' he said placatingly.

'That's not the point.'

'You object to living in the lap of luxury?'

'No, what I do object to is——'

'You like the sunshine?'

'Yes.'

'Count your blessings,' he advised. 'Plenty of girls would give their eye teeth to be where you are now. Agreed?'

Clemence sighed. Living with Howard, she had learned when arguing had a future and when it had none. Now she was wasting her breath. 'I guess so.'

'Then you'll clear an extra slug with the boy boss? Thanks, you're a pal. If an additional day or two needs to be tacked on at the end, we'll sort that out later.' He was speaking at a rush, which both held her protests at bay and restrained the galloping telephone bill. 'Smile nicely, show a bit of leg. Young Khalid has all the makings of a ladies' man. He'd like nothing better than to whip you off to his harem.'

'Rubbish,' she managed to insert, but he went rattling on.

'Must go—Yvonne's waiting outside in the car, and she'll be wondering where I've got to. You caught us on the point of driving over to take another look at a music shop which is for sale. It's what we'd like, a thriving business in a good area with living accommodation above, and——' Yet again, Howard coughed. 'Actually I've gone ahead and put down a deposit. It's eaten up all my available funds, which means the cash you're bringing in is vital. After calling at the shop we're taking off for a couple of days.'

'I understood you were broke,' Clemence said scathingly.

'Not quite. 'Bye.'

He ended the call, leaving her with a load of questions unasked. Like where had he and his girlfriend been of late? Like how could she contact him over the next few days? Like was his mother—in reality a hyperactive sixty-year-old—supposed to be recovering, fading, or dead? And what had he told Khalid in the first place? Feverishly Clemence instructed the switchboard to reconnect her, but when the number rang out the next time there was no reply. She had been suspended in limbo, or could it be left out on a limb? Both, she decided. Which meant she was horribly vulnerable to whatever Jassim Al Fori chose to throw at her next.

CHAPTER THREE

THE following evening Clemence was half-way through her selection of tunes from musicals, past and present, when Jassim walked into the lobby. Her stomach knotted. That morning the need to clear Howard's extended furlough had had her up and breakfasted at an indecently early hour. Then she had waited for Khalid. And waited. More dilatory than usual, the young man had not appeared until noon, by which time she was feeling stale, fractious and one hundred per cent the fraud. Oozing smiles, and despising herself every inch of the way, she had explained that her partner required a further ten days' grace. Her embarrassment was great, but would it be possible? Please.

'Happy to oblige,' the young Arab had said, carelessly accepting her fudged account of an improvement in her mother-in-law's health.

But Jassim would accept nothing. When his five-minute span grew into ten, fifteen, twenty minutes, she realised he must have been primed with the facts and was waiting to take her to task. The knots in her stomach tightened. And when he strode over at the end of her performance, she felt positively cramped.

'Your mother-in-law did wreck the timetable.' He pushed the slouch hat from his brow. 'As anticipated.'

'The situation's fluid, but she has rallied a little.' Clemence's rehearsed reply was defiant. 'Howard and I are delighted.'

'Do you and your husband keep in constant touch?' he enquired, his look advising a steadfast suspicion of anything she might say. 'If so, you must be spending a fortune. I ring Brisbane on a regular basis and it damn near cripples me.'

'We don't, we're not,' she said, plucking at the waist of the white satin top worn with baggy trousers. She refused to be fooled. Aha, she thought, you've checked with the switchboard and know that, despite the flurry of attempts to make contact, Howard and I have spoken to each other exactly once. 'Before he left we agreed calls should be kept to a minimum,' she continued, by way of an explanation. 'We're saving hard to—to buy a house.'

She received a cool green glance. 'The cash you're raking in here should finance a down payment on Buckingham Palace.'

In truth Clemence half agreed, but she was not going to tell him that. Instead she jammed her music folder beneath her arm and set off across the lobby at a rate of knots. What happens this evening? she thought when he kept pace. Another grilling for certain, but was there to be more, 'Keep your hands off junior'? Another kiss? She drew up short before the doors which led out on to the terrace. 'Must you shadow me like this?' she demanded.

Jassim folded his arms, rested his weight on one leg, and took his time to answer. 'Yes.'

'But why? I've done nothing wrong, and I've no intention of doing anything wrong.'

'No? Let me put it this way. You're a married woman, yet last night you impaled yourself on me and proceeded to kiss me. Wasn't that wrong?'

Clemence gazed at him. She was not safe with this man. He had taken the truth and juggled it around to suit himself.

'You kissed me!' she protested, her face crimson. Then felt the compulsion to insist, 'And left me cold.'

'That's not what it seemed like at the time.'

'I was . . . startled.'

He grunted, and the grunt indicated two things: one, she had given a lame excuse; two, to him the kiss had not mattered a damn. She wished it hadn't mattered to her.

'Ditto,' he said. 'However, one area where we differ is the fact that I'm unattached, which is a damned sight more than can be said for you, *Mrs* Harrell.'

How tempting it was to blurt out the truth. Yet Clemence suspected that if she revealed her single status he would then do his best to have her booted out of the country. Mean tricks could be Jassim Al Fori's strong point. No, here she was and here she would do her utmost to stay. Even if it meant sleeping with one eye open. Why should she allow this two-bit swashbuckler to part her from a contract which, as he had pointed out himself, was lucrative in the extreme? Howard was depending on the money, and although his allegiance had shifted she did owe him some consideration—for old times' sake if nothing else. But it was not only her partner who would benefit. When Harrell & Co was disbanded, she planned to continue her career alone. But how much work would be available to a solo harpist? Plenty? Some? Little? Over the years Clemence had put money away, but if her savings could be boosted survival during any thin patch would be eased.

'Are Harrell & Co in the habit of receiving a king's ransom in return for their services?' Jassim enquired, demonstrating a flair for telepathy.

'No,' she admitted. He must know full well they were a long way from the Liberace bracket, so why feed him unnecessary lies? The truth had been bent far too much already.

'You're not hot properties?'

'Lukewarm at best.'

Unexpectedly he grinned, the vertical dimple creasing a

cheek which, as on the previous evening, was smooth-shaven. His clothes might give testimony to the ruffian, but his razor had been put to good use.

'I understood folk in your line plumped up their reputations, not trimmed them down,' he commented. 'But don't undersell yourself, you're dynamite on that harp.'

A warm glow started, only to be quickly tempered. Because he had paid her a compliment, there was no need to act as if it were Christmas. Even so, Clemence heard herself saying garrulously, 'Our agent received a call out of the blue, asking for us. The terms offered were so fantastic there was no way we could refuse.'

Jassim digested the information. 'I don't suppose you've met Khalid before?' he asked.

'No. How could I? This is my first time in Oman.'

'He had a couple of weeks in London last year with his mother. If you didn't remember Khalid, you'd remember her. Leyla's been in Paris for the past month, so you won't have seen her around, but she's a dramatic-looking woman—dark hair, dark eyes, and dressed by Yves St Laurent. When she walks into a room everybody takes notice, or if they don't, she wants to know why,' he drawled, his mouth crooking with irony. 'It must have been March when Mrs Al Fori and her beloved boychild honoured London with their presence.'

Clemence thought back. 'Last March Howard and I were in Rome.'

'A romantic city, Rome. Great place for a honeymoon.' He slid her a glance. 'How long have you been married?'

She went from vroom-vroom to putt-putt. 'Um, three years.'

'You don't sound too sure.'

'I am,' Clemence insisted, feeling skewered.

'I notice you don't wear a wedding-ring.'

'I—I lost it a few weeks ago.'

'Do you and your husband have one of those open-style marriages? You know, you go your way, he goes his, and there are no recriminations?'

'Pass,' she blazed. 'My private life has nothing to do with you. My God! You'd just love to be able to tie me to a chair and train a spotlight in my eyes, wouldn't you?'

'It's an idea,' he replied, with what could have been a hint of a grin.

'You've yet to get round to it, but to save you the bother of asking you'll be pleased to hear that the sum total of my contact with Khalid today amounts to sixty seconds. However,' Clemence declared, 'I did eat two men for breakfast.'

'Dieting?'

'Starvation rations.'

If it had been a grin, it had vanished. 'You are aware adultery is regarded as a grave offence over here?'

'Then it's just as well I won't be committing any!'

Her forcefulness hit home, in so much as Jassim frowned, rubbing his chin.

'Mrs Harrell——' he began.

'My name's Clemence, and I'm not a *femme fatale* by any stretch of the imagination. I accept that my stage clothes are sometimes ... flash, but they're worn to project an image.'

'The image being wham-bam sexy?'

'The image being glamour. With a soupçon of sex,' she concurred, noting a disbelieving curve to his mouth.

It's a soup *bowl*,' he declared, and grinned. It was a killer of a grin, full of fun. A grin which had her temper fizzling away.

'I don't relish a spat with you every day from now until I leave, so can't we call a truce?' pleaded Clemence, taking advantage of this unexpected patch of sunshine. 'I give you my word I'm not the least bit interested in Khalid, or any other man, come to that.'

'You're only interested in your husband?'

'Yes.' How she wished she had remembered to say that herself, first.

His slouch hat was removed and the brim scrutinised. 'What form would this truce take?'

'An end to your daily patrols, of course.'

'I'm not convinced that would be wise,' Jassim said evenly.

Clemence groaned. 'Have you any idea how my performance suffers from the knowledge that you're going to appear and dissect me?' she implored. 'My harp-playing is not enriched.'

'It's best that I come. For the moment.' He stopped examining his hat and raised it to his head to grin. 'But in future I could hum along, whistle through my fingers, stamp my feet?' he suggested, his Australian twang pronounced. 'Or even stand on stage beside you, swaying to the music and chanting "Oowa-diddy-diddy-oowa"?'

'No, thank you.'

'Suppose I huddle deep in my corner and be self-effacing?'

'You'd be about as self-effacing as a tarantula in the bath!'

Jassim gave a mock wince. 'I'm not that much of a turn-off, am I?'

'Yes!'

'You wound me.'

'Your daily patrols wound me,' Clemence declared. 'My definition of a truce means your cloak-and-dagger antics must cease. Come six o'clock each evening, you're not to be anywhere near me.'

'And if I refuse?'

A cloud came over the sun.

'Then I shall do my own thing,' she said, trying to appear mysterious, but instead hearing herself sound vinegary.

'Go ahead, do your own thing. But don't forget, I shall be watching you and——' the green eyes glittered. '—awaiting developments with bated breath.'

True to his word, Jassim arrived the next evening. This time, however, he restricted his visit to the regulation five minutes and did not linger to ask questions. Contrarily, Clemence found herself wishing he had. Separate him from his distrust and he showed signs of being an eminently reasonable personality, which implied that his suspicions must be rooted in solid motivation. But what motivation? Unless they talked her chances of finding out were nil.

The days which followed were boosted by her anticipation of the outing with Otto, but when he rolled up on her doorstep on Thursday morning one look at his woeful expression advised that the outing was at risk.

'Hate to let you down like this,' he apologised, 'but for a long time now I've been troubled with toothache, and——' he cupped a hand around his jaw, '—it's grown progressively worse. I need to have the tooth seen to, and the only time the dentist can take me is to-day.'

'Don't worry about it,' Clemence had assured him.

'We'll refix the outing for next Thursday.'

She hid her disappointment and nodded.

From then on, the time was relentlessly filled. She added new tunes to her repertoire, embarked on a rigorous exercise regime, read voraciously—and grew to know every stick and stone of the tiny fishing village off by heart. Howard did not ring, but Khalid and Otto stopped by to talk. And so did Jassim.

He marked up attendance each evening, and although his patrol could be an in-and-out affair, on several occasions he had arrived as her act was finishing and walked over. Each time his conversation had been short and restricted to her music. Demanding an explanation for his attitude had not been possible. Yet he had been pleasant, often humorous. His distrust had been well concealed, so much so that Clemence had found herself thinking that seeing the sights with him would have been more fun than with dull old Otto. But the Swiss was her escort, and by Tuesday the outing had begun to loom large again.

Clemence was hurrying towards the bar, where her show was due to start within minutes, when Khalid waylaid her.

'There's a barbecue tomorrow evening. Will you come?'

'I'd love to,' she smiled, glancing across at a poster which advertised the Plaza's weekly 'gala night'. 'But with two performances to give, I wouldn't have sufficient time.'

'May I offer a solution? If you have no objections, I would like to cancel your second show tomorrow. An Indian group have been at me hammer and—sickle?'

'Hammer and tongs.'

'Yes.' He fingered his beard. 'They've been begging me to give them a chance, and tomorrow would seem a perfect time for them to—test the water?'

Clemence nodded, agreeing both with the phrase and with the suggestion. She was not so all-consumed with the impact of her music that one missed performance mattered. She wished the Indians well, and told him so.

'Thanks. So as you'll be free, I shall escort you to the barbecue,' Khalid stated. 'For two days now a business conference has occupied me, but tomorrow I shall kick up my feet.'

'Heels.'

'Heels. I'll collect you after your first session. Will that be suitable?'

'Sounds fine.'

At last life was beginning to sparkle, Clemence decided as she practised her harp the next day. Otto had an itinerary planned for tomorrow's travels, while this evening she was dining out gala-style. Although their schedule meant she and Howard had never been able to attend the barbecues, they had drooled over the possibility. Each week the chef featured the cuisine from a different country. Would this be Italian night, the tables sagging beneath crocks of spaghetti and lasagne? Or would the waiters don straw hats, serve drinks in half-coconuts and food Polynesian style? Maybe a smörgasbörd would be set out beneath the stars? Whatever the slant, the prospect was exciting.

When Jassim arrived at six o'clock, Clemence awarded him a megawatt smile. She could tell he was surprised, but he recovered quickly and smiled back across the heads of the people in the foyer. I could like you, she decided, as his dimple twitched, and when, five minutes later, he wiggled his fingers and mouthed what seemed suspiciously like 'Cheerio, sunshine,' she almost laughed out loud. Why had she ever seen a similarity to a white hunter? Jassim was a guardian angel, and she lived in heaven. How different eveything seemed, simply because an event or two had stumbled on to her horizon!

'Ready?' enquired Khalid, appearing as she picked her way down from the stage.

'Not quite. I need to call in at the bungalow to change, but it won't take five minutes.'

His face fell. 'Why change?'

'You don't expect me to mooch around all evening in this, do you?' Clemence asked with a laugh.

This was a catsuit in shiny cloth-of-gold, a slice of pure showbiz schmaltz. The wide-shouldered top had a tendency to open and close in a most tantalising way, so to be on the safe side she had worn a sequinned jacket. She was well covered, even if the suit did cling. Totally impractical, walking in the outfit required care, and the three-inch-high cobweb of golden straps which passed for sandals made movement even more precarious.

'Leave it on, for me,' Khalid pleaded.

'I'd rather not,' she said, but her objection went unheeded as the young Arab clasped her elbow and began hurrying her towards the main exit. 'Shouldn't we go that way?' she enquired, looking back at the glass doors which led onto the gardens.

He winked. 'Wait and see.' Past the doorman and out on to the covered porch he propelled her. Indicating a low-slung purple sports car with yellow number plates, he grinned. 'Jump in.'

'Isn't the barbecue held on the lawn between the pool and the tennis courts? said Clemence, eyes wide with question. Had she misunderstood his invitation? she began to wonder. Was this yet another breakdown in communications?

'We're not going to the Plaza's barbecue. I'm taking you to one being held further along the coast.' Khalid peeled off his jacket and went round to the driver's door. 'Jump in,' he coaxed again. 'You don't want to keep everybody waiting.'

Everybody? Clemence tumbled to what was happening. The youth must have arranged a get-together with his friends, and intended to dazzle them by arriving with her clad in her flamboyant stage gear. The idea was adolescent, but—she sighed—if it boosted his ego to have her in tow like some Cannes film festival starlet, so be it. Khalid had co-operated in full when Howard had broken the terms of their contract, which made it churlish not to co-operate with him now.

'Jumping' into the sports car proved an impossibility. A slow motion version of the Fosbury Flop was required before Clemence could manoeuvre herself in beside him. Smiling gratefully when her escort leant over to buckle the safety harness, she was even more grateful before they had reached the end of the drive. Khalid's driving style was also adolescent. He shot out from the porch, narrowly missing a reversing limousine and terrifying a man on the joggers' circuit which ran parallel. The evening sky was magenta darkening into midnight blue, but he paid no attention to diminished visibility, nor to the traffic. Gaining the highway, he overtook everything, usually at the expense of oncoming vehicles whose drivers presented fast-forwards of terrified eyes and mute screams of terror. A red and white oil drum, one of many demarcating roadworks, was clipped and rolled away, booming dementedly.

'How far are we going?' Clemence questioned.

'Not far.'

How far is not far? she wanted to ask, but at her query Khalid had turned to smile, and to risk him taking his eyes off the road again seemed highly unwise. They passed a football stadium ablaze with lights, then sped on to a flyover, constructed in a groove blasted through a hillside. At the hotel daily-watered lawns and massed blossoms had flourished, but this landscape was harsh and dry. Clinging on to the safety strap which crossed between her breasts, Clemence decided that if these were to be her final moments, she might as well see all she could see. Off the flyover, they sped down through a small town. Onion-domed mosques, shops plastered with flowing Arabic script, white cube houses half-hidden behind whitewashed walls, flashed by. This visual proof that she was in a foreign

land had her blue-grey eyes swinging to right and to left.
Everything intrigued. Everything looked *different*. An
adrenalin rush of excitement replaced her adrenalin rush of
fear. Tomorrow Otto will show me all this in daylight,
Clemence thought, and grinned.

Rapidly, the town became a memory. The highway
skirted barren hills, ran across a dark and empty plain.
Then around another hill. Many miles, but not too many
minutes later, Khalid swung off the tarmacadam and
dipped down on to a potholed and stony track which she
decided must be a *wadi*, a dried-up river bed. Along they
shot through a moonlit wilderness of sand and gravel, while
Clemence's heart bumped and banged around in sympathy
with the lurchings of the car. Respect for suspension would
have slowed most drivers, but the young man's foot stayed
down hard. With a squeal of tyres, they swerved up the
bank of the water course and headed for a rocky outcrop,
entering a gorge where walls towered darkly up on either
side, an arm's stretch away. She held her breath. Given
their speed, disaster seemed imminent, and when the car
eventually emerged into the open and stopped, she felt
weak.

Struggling out as Khalid opened her door, she stood up
and looked around. He had brought her to a tiny, picture-
postcard bay. Cupped by a craggy rock fingers at either
end, the slender arc of silver sand was as pure as icing sugar.
A solitary palm tree rustled in the evening breeze, and she
heard the suck and retreat of baby waves as they giggled
among themselves.

'It's beautiful!' she enthused.

'Not as beautiful as you.' Khalid caught hold of her hand
and raised it to his lips. 'Your beauty reminds me of a
magnolia, a bud with petals which will open and enfold.'

Clemence gave him a despairing look. Which book did

you read that in? she was tempted to ask. The young man in Rome had had her wincing at his fanciful compliments, but in Khalid he could have a rival. Yet to find her escort acting the smitten swain was unexpected. Admittedly he had paid extravagant compliments before, had shown by his smiles how much he liked her, but his attentions had seemed more those of a chum than anything heavier. Now his gaze and the way his fingers continued to curl around hers spoke of the fervent. For some reason, Khalid had succumbed to a fit of romance.

'Thank you,' she said, retrieving her hand.

She made to stride briskly ahead, but one step had her high heels disappearing into the sand. A second, and she was in danger of overbalancing. She was bending down to remove her sandals when a movement caught her eye, and she gave a gasp of delight. A hundred yards or so away, in a shadowy cleft, a Bedouin tent had been pitched. Before it, on the sand, flamed an orange fire, and tending the blaze was a white-robed figure, his head covered by a maroon-tasselled *shemag*, the standard Omani headdress. The scene was so impossibly Arabian Nights that if Sinbad the Sailor had chosen that moment to leap from the rocks and charge down to the inky swell of the ocean, Clemence would not have been surprised.

'You entertain in style,' she praised.

'Ingrid and I enjoyed our assignation in the tent,' the young man said, visibly preening. 'I guessed you would like it, too.'

'Who's Ingrid?'

'A friend, like you are my friend,' he murmured, and was off again, showering compliments like wedding rice.

Sandals dangling from her fingers, Clemence walked by his side. The heat of the day had gone, and a breeze sifted gently through her hair. Beneath her feet, the sand felt soft.

A perfect place, a perfect evening, she thought, as lights winked on a fishing *dhow* far out at sea. Khalid was comparing her hair to 'golden strands spun by heavenly silkworms' when her stomach rumbled. So much for perfection! She was hungry. Then it dawned that something was missing. Shouldn't there be the aroma of grilling steaks, the sizzle of sausages? Where was the food, but more to the point, where were the people?

'I don't see any other guests,' she said, recalling how their car had been parked in solitary slendour.

'There are no other guests.' Khalid smiled his cherubic smile. 'This evening is for the two of us. Mahmoud will stand guard. Just a precaution, you understand? But have no fear, he can be trusted.'

Maybe your servant's full of sterling qualities, but how about you? Clemence found herself wondering as Khalid called a few words of Arabic which resulted in the robed man leaving the fire and fading away into the night.

'Earlier you referred to "everybody",' she said, tackling him head on. 'You deliberately gave the impression we were joining a crowd. Sorry, but I don't appreciate being tricked.'

'No tricks,' he grinned. 'Just a —white lie? And now you are mine, to do with as I wish. As Howard said.'

'I'm sure he did not,' she objected, as the youth reached out and caught hold of her by the waist.

'Yes. When I asked would he mind if I talked with you, became your friend, his words were——' he quoted, '"Don't worry about me. Clemence is all yours. Take her".'

'He didn't mean it literally!' She pressed her hands against his chest to prevent the embrace she saw coming, but to little effect. Short and slightly-built as he was, Khalid proved to be strong. His arms tightened around her, and he nuzzled into her neck. 'You've got it wrong,' she insisted, grimacing as his beard scraped. 'Howard was using a figure of speech.'

'You have such a lovely figure—high breasts, slender waist, curvy hips. Let me look.' Before she could stop him, he had dragged the jacket from her shoulders and flung it on to the sand. 'Such a lovely figure,' he repeated, drinking in the pout of her tanned breasts. 'I shall see more when we bathe naked in the ocean.'

'If you think I'm going skinny-dipping with you, you can think again!'

'Skinny-dipping?' The young Arab frowned, then his face cleared. 'Ah, you are frightened of sea snakes? OK, we are naked in the tent.'

'We are not!'

Trapped against him, Clemence began to curse herself for her lack of foresight, her foolishness. She had allowed herself to be driven out into the wilderness by a youth whose behaviour indicated that he had mistaken her common-or-garden cordiality for something else. And who had taken Howard's cavalier statements as readings from the Gospel. Too late, she recalled another of his statements—about the boy wanting to whip her off to a harem. A harem seemed obscure, but the reason for bringing her to this remote beach was crystal clear.

'Khalid, I'm not interested in . . . messing around,' she told him starchily.

'Yes, you are,' he said, and chuckled.

'*No!*'

Clemence made a determined effort to break his hold, but to no effect. He refused to let her go. She tried again, batting at his arms and voicing her disapproval, but he simply held on tighter and chuckled, chuckled, chuckled. Another unsuccessful struggle, and sparks of incipient panic ignited. Until then she had been apprehensive, yet sure he could be made to see reason. His laughter changed everything. Khalid was no longer a harmless youth, he had become a coldly calculating wolf. The entire evening, the tent, the guard, must have been planned in advance, like a military operation. And this general was determined to win.

'Fight, my bud,' he encouraged. 'Ingrid used to fight, but I plucked her. Like I shall pluck you.'

'Never!' Clemence fought to escape the squirm of the male body against hers, the hot breath in her face. His hands had begun to move; dabbing into her cleavage, searching for the zip of her catsuit. 'Help!' she shouted, though she knew any appeal would be useless. The servant wasn't going to intervene, and chances of the distant fishing boat bestirring itself and chugging to her rescue were infinitesimal.

'You don't want help,' chuckled Khalid. 'I know the— how do you say?—foibles of Western women. I know how much they love to fight and tease. That way surrender is all the sweeter. Carry on fighting, my passionate bud.'

'I'm not passionate,' she gasped, straining back as far as she could.

'No? You might look as demure as apple pie, but I've seen that sway to your hips.'

'You're talking nonsense.' Clemence summoned up what she hoped was a note of authority. 'I demand to be taken back to the hotel, this minute!'

'Later, much later. In two or three days' time.'

He had begun shuffling her towards the tent, an arm caught behind her back, and now she wrenched around her head to gaze at him.

'Two or three days?' she bleated.

'I told you, I shall kick up my feet.'

'Heels,' Clemence corrected automatically.

'Whatever. And once you've discovered how expertly I can handle a woman, two or three days will not seem long enough. Later tonight I shall drive you to a secret hideaway, and there we'll come together time and time again. You will discover the truth in the saying that it is Arabs who make the best lovers.'

Clemence detested his cocksure confidence, the way he smirked. How could she get it through to him that she was not up for grabs?

'I realise you think Howard gave me to you, but you're mistaken,' she began. 'On the contrary, if he knew what you were doing he'd——'

'He wouldn't care,' Khalid interrupted, and held the tent flap aside.

When Clemence's eyes adjusted to the gloom, she realised she had been delivered into what could best be described as a ruby-red—and innately Arabic—womb. The tent walls and roof had been draped in crimson gauze, while plush *dhurries* covered the sand to add a kasbah touch. On one side embroidered pillows in dusky pink and scarlet lay in an inviting heap. Beneath the mellow glow of an oil lamp, she saw two low tables of beaten copper; one was filled with dishes of olives, nuts and sweetmeats, the other bore a brass coffee-pot and cups. The air was heavy with the fragrance of roses which floated from a silver burner. In different circumstances this lovers' retreat would have enchanted her, now Clemence was filled with horror.

'Please, you don't understand,' she began, as Khalid twisted her to face him. This way and that she moved, trying to thwart his demands, but he seemed to be all around, chuckling, fevered, tenacious.

He said words in Arabic, then continued in his chocolatey English, 'Do you act the tease with your other lovers, dear heart? Do you drive them to a frenzy before you open up?'

'I don't have other lovers. Ouch!' she exclaimed, when his teeth nipped at the lobe of her ear.

'You don't like that? Ingrid did.'

'I'm not Ingrid, whoever she is, and I object to being bitten. I also object to being called dear heart. But most of all, I object to having been brought here.'

'You don't like the beach?' The cherubic features were puzzled. 'OK, we drive to my hideaway.'

'No!'

If Khalid managed to get her inside a house, she would be his prisoner and patently in dire straits. Clemence realised she must escape and now. If her memory was correct, he had left the car keys in the ignition, so . . . How did she free herself? Fighting like a maenad was useless. Think. Think. Think. She forced herself to go limp. She smiled and touched his cheek. Khalid grinned. Capitulation—if he had known the word he would have said it out loud. He had relaxed his guard and begun murmuring words of Arabic when Clemence raised her leg and kneed him in the groin as hard as she could. In an instant, the endearments switched to curses. Khalid staggered back, his face contorted with pain and astonishment.

From the tent she fled, and along the beach. She ran and ran, but it was like a bad dream; one of those where no matter how fast you go, you get nowhere. The icing sugar sand had turned to glue, and despite the frantic pounding of her feet, the ache in her lungs which insisted she must be moving at speed, there seemed scant progress. The hundred yards back to the car had become a hundred miles. If only she had been wearing shirt and shorts, instead of a skintight catsuit!

On she sprinted, until at last a low shape appeared

among the shadows. Clemence was swerving towards it
when she heard a strangled shout of Arabic. Behind her
came the thud of feet, the sound of heavy breathing.
Someone was in pursuit. A swift glance over her shoulder,
and she caught sight of the servant. Middle-aged the man
might be, but he moved nimbly. His arm had been raised,
and he was holding aloft something which glinted in the
moonlight. Clemence stumbled, recovered, ran harder than
ever. The servant had worn a silver *khanjar* in his belt, so
what he was brandishing could only be a dagger! Heart
almost exploding with fear, she charged off on to the harder
sand where Khalid had parked. One grab at the handle,
and she flung herself into the driving-seat. A seam ripped,
but she took no notice. If every inch of the cloth-of-gold had
been torn from her back, she would not have cared. Escape
was all. Sweat glossing her brow, breath coming short and
quick, she fumbled with the key. A flash of white through
the windscreen warned that the servant was drawing near.

'Thank you, thank you,' gurgled Clemence, when the
engine roared into life.

Crashing into gear, any gear, she circled in the tightest,
fastest turn she had ever made. If the wheels became
bogged down, she was lost. Spraying up sand in two
gigantic wings, the car shot round and sped into the gorge.
Fate was on her side. A thread away from hysteria,
Clemence hooted with raucous laughter. She was safe!

Relief lived a short life. Mere seconds later, she saw lights
ahead and her eyes widened, the pupils dilating in alarm. A
vehicle was being driven towards her. Somehow Khalid
had called in reinforcements. Exuberance collapsed into
despair. The gorge was too narrow to allow two vehicles to
pass by, so what did she do? Force a head-on collision or
admit defeat? The choice was no choice. She stamped on the
brake and brought the car shuddering to a halt. Switching

off the engine, she folded her arms across the steering-wheel and sank down her head. She felt like death. The lights came nearer and nearer. The vehicle stopped. There was a moment or two of silence, then the door beside her opened. Anticipation held her rigid. Now she would be taken back to Khalid. Now she would be forced to submit.

'What's happening here?' asked a voice with a twang, and she looked up to see a dark-haired man in an ancient shirt and jeans frowning in at her.

'Jassim!'

No particular logic told her he had come to her rescue, Clemence just knew. She crawled out of the car and into his arms.

CHAPTER FOUR

'THANK goodness you're here!' she babbled, pushing her head into the most comforting shoulder she had ever known. She wrapped her arms around his neck and held on tight. 'Khalid said he was bringing me to a barbecue, but instead I'm—I'm attacked!'

'You've been hurt?' Jassim sounded wary.

'No,' Clemence wailed. In the past she had denounced Yvonne's habit of weeping at the slightest excuse with a scalding incredulity, and was now amazed to find herself dripping salt tears down his shirt. She gave a series of unladylike sniffs. 'But it was a near thing. You see, he has a knife.'

'Khalid has a knife?' he demanded, catching hold of her arms and unwinding them.

'No, his servant. He was trying to stab me.'

Jassim shook his head. 'Mahmoud wouldn't hurt a fly.'

The denial came like a smack in the mouth. Clemence had not expected to be contradicted, she had somehow expected condolences, understanding, tender loving care. Now she scowled as it registered that, in addition to contradicting her claim, he had firmly broken all contact, just when she needed to be close. She rubbed at her cheeks, diverting mascara rivers into muddy blotches.

'He was going to hurt me!' she declared, indignation lifting her voice to glass-shattering level.

Jassim frowned. 'Are you sure?'

'Certain.'

Abruptly he reached out and took hold of her shoulders to swivel her around. The servant was approaching along the gorge, a ghostly figure in billowing white robes. Chest rising and falling, the rasp of his breath made a harsh sound. Dumbly Clemence stared. The only thing he carried was a pair of sandals, metallic gold sandals which shone in the moonlight.

'You seem to be confused,' Jassim told her, dragging a crumpled handkerchief from his trouser pocket. 'Here, for heaven's sake blow your nose.'

If he hadn't sounded so patronising maybe she would have admitted her mistake, but his casual manner served to harden her mood. Clemence was not prepared to be treated lightly. He must be made to recognise the trauma she had gone through, then he would be properly sympathetic. She blew her nose and had started into a graphic, if garbled, denunciation of Khalid and his confederate when she became aware that Jassim had switched his gaze to the servant. His interest was straying. Her tirade petered out as he discarded her with no more than a nod and took the man to one side. The Arabic exchange was incomprehensible, but one thing she understood—the attention she craved was being despatched wholesale. A hand spread on Mahmoud's shoulder, Jassim displayed an avid interest in every word he uttered. But he should have been listening to her! How dare he treat her plight in such an offhand fashion, and now be fascinated by whatever it was Mahmoud had to say? Her rush into his arms had been in the unswerving belief that a guardian angel had arrived. But Jassim Al Fori could never be typecast as anyone's guardian angel, especially hers! From first sight he had been critical, and now she possessed proof that he was also soulless, unfeeling and——

'Come along.' He beckoned as though she were a thumb-sucking toddler. 'We'll go and sort this out with Khalid. I understand you've left him writhing on the ground with tears in his eyes.' His mouth twitched. 'Let's hope you haven't ruined his prospects for all time!'

Clemence took a step backwards. There was no way she could confront Khalid, not right now. Didn't Jassim realise the memory of being mauled was too stark, too recent? Was he totally bereft of sensitivity?

'No!' Her hair swirled around her head. 'I want nothing more to do with that brother of yours. He's a brute, a lecher. He should be castrated!'

'Sounds drastic,' Jassim commented, and threw back his head and laughed.

Clemence's hysteria ebbed. She forgot all about being upset. Now she was purely and simply furious. 'I'm glad you think it's funny,' she snapped. 'Let's see if the police are equally amused when the details are reported to them!'

In a flash his laughter was replaced by a grim expression. 'There's no need for the police to be involved.' Spoken by anyone else in the same situation, the words might have sounded coaxing, persuasive, even a touch like a plea. Coming from Jassim they were firm, just firm.

'I disagree.' She poked the handkerchief at him. 'I'm sure they'll be very interested to know that your brother's a lascivious, over-sexed monster who preys on women.'

'Women?' He grimaced at the sodden ball before pushing it gingerly back into his pocket. 'Plural?'

'Woman, then. Khalid's pure Jekyll and Hyde—cute boyish charm one moment, and the next he molests me. I'll tell it all to the police,' Clemence reiterated.

'Let's stop playing games, shall we?'

'Games?'

Jassim sat his hands on his hips. 'What stunt are you pulling? Is it blackmail? It must be—what else?' His anger erupted like a Cape Wrath storm. 'Of course, you're in show business, so I should have guessed you do a little acting on the side. And tears come cheap. Have you studied drama? Whether or not, you're good—Oscar standard. The anguish in those big blue eyes of yours almost had me fooled.' Heat and humidity had twisted the hair at the back of his neck into tight curls long ago, and he thrust a hand through them, massaging roughly. 'Don't be shy,' he sneered. 'State your terms. What's your price for keeping quiet—a purse full of *rials*, or would you prefer payment in gold?'

'I don't know what you're talking about,' Clemence protested.

'Why don't you come clean, for once?' His look hit ten degrees below terminal frostbite. 'Why don't you admit that your aim from the start was to set Khalid up? I was awaiting developments, but this is incredible. Pure copycat. God Almighty! it appears to be *de rigueur* for types like you to——'

'Your basic premise is wrong,' she cut in.

'What basic premise?'

'That I'm a type. I'm not. I'm an individual—I'm me.'

Penetrating green eyes scuffed over her.

'Congratulations,' he drawled.

'Thank you. And may I congratulate you on being the most cynical mine of misinformation I've ever been unlucky enough to meet. Your accusations are ridiculous. I came here in good faith, never imagining for one minute it was Khalid's intention to leap on me.'

'That's your story, and you're sticking to it?'

'Yes!' she stormed.

'I imagine you think you're beautifully blameless, but it would be wise to bear in mind that the police might also be interested to hear a few home truths about you.' Jassim's voice dropped, becoming very soft, very dangerous. 'They'd find it interesting to know how you allowed Khalid to buy you drinks and encouraged his friendship. And how you joined him at night on a deserted beach, dressed in what appear to be leftovers from the Folies Bergére.'

Ready to object, her denials were left for later as her eyes followed the downward plunge of his. The seam which had torn as she had hurled herself into the car had been a side seam. To her dismay, Clemence saw her catsuit gaping open beneath her armpit, almost down to her waist. That she was naked beneath did not require confirmation.

'These are my stage clothes,' she defended, clamping the material together with her fingers. She threw a look at the servant, daring him to react, but he was propped up against the rock face with eyes closed, resting.

'Wonderful excuse,' derided Jassim. 'Try telling that to a judge and jury, or anyone else for that matter. Roll up at a police station in that outfit, and——'

'I had a jacket until your brother ripped it off me. And if you think I'd blackmail anyone, you're crazy!' Clemence told him, reverting to the earlier slur. 'I don't want anything from Khalid.' In truth, she was not exactly sure what she wanted any more. A show of sympathy would have been nice, but retribution? Reporting the incident to the police had been a wild idea, thrown in in a fit of pique with no intention of following through. But even if she had wanted to air her grievances, bringing herself to the notice of the authorities would be unwise. As Howard had warned, she must keep a low profile. 'I was bought one drink,' she said, veering off, 'and that was a fruit juice. What's more, I've never strung him along or encouraged his friendship. He was chatty, so I was chatty in return. I don't regard that as an offence against humanity.'

'In my book any married woman who plays around the minute her husband's back is turned deserves all she gets.'

'I've not been playing around,' Clemence retorted, hands awkwardly stapled beneath her armpit.

'You were brought here by force tonight?'

'No, but——'

'So you agreed to this meeting.' His voice throbbed with disdain. 'Why don't we cut the——' Jassim thought better.

'Do yourself a favour, sunshine, quit the pretence of outraged virgin and admit you've been leading young Khalid up the garden path.'

'I've led him *nowhere*.'

Her protest went unheeded.

'In Khalid you saw a way to get rich quick. He represented a lifetime exit from playing music in hotel bars.'

'That's not true!' Clemence cast around for a way of convincing him of her innocence. One crux of his accusation was the belief that she was married, so how about announcing her spinsterhood? That would burst his balloon. Yet the revelation could provoke more problems than it solved. Considering her dubious legality in Oman, she would be foolish to blow her cover. And even if she did, making a bald statement would never be enough. Jassim would revert to interrogation, and before she knew what was happening she might find herself being forced to admit to Howard's real reason for going home. What her censor would make of that little revelation, she shuddered to think. 'I did not lead Khalid anywhere,' she repeated, each word clipped. 'It was the other way around. He's the culprit, I'm the victim.'

The terminal frostbite was reduced to an icy glare.

'You're over twenty-one. When he suggested coming here you must have suspected——'

'I climbed into his car on the understanding that I was being taken to a barbecue. I see now that as wise moves go it left much to be desired, but I suspected *nothing*.'

Deep in thought, Jassim surveyed her. A full minute seemed to trundle by before he next spoke. 'It goes against the grain to disbelieve a lovely girl,' he said at last, 'so, for the time being, I'm prepared to give you the benefit of the doubt, Mrs Harrell.'

'That's handsome of you, Mr Al Fori!'

'My friends call me Jass.'

'And what do your enemies call you?' enquired Clemence, flinging him a look which would have turned milk sour at fifty paces. 'Where I come from it's possible for a girl to go for a drive with someone without suspecting them of dastardly deeds, and that's what I did this evening. I——'

'OK, OK, calm down! Whatever's happened, shall we forget it? I regret you've been manhandled, but Mahmoud tells me Khalid came off far worse. Be assured, he won't approach you again.' A laconic smile tipped his mouth to one side. 'I doubt he'll be fit enough to approach anyone for a while. You may even have put him off women for life.'

'That seems unlikely.' Relieved that his mud-slinging had ceased, Clemence remained a long way from feeling satisfied. His remark about giving her the benefit of the doubt was no prize, because nothing had been retracted. Jassim had not said whether he believed her denials or not. One minute he had been accusing her of leading Khalid astray, the next he had backed off. Why the quick change? Something did not jell. 'Who's Ingrid?' she asked.

A sinew moved in his jaw. 'Why? What has Khalid said about her?'

'Nothing much, but——'

'Ingrid's of no consequence.' All of a sudden he was impatient to go. 'We've wasted enough time here. You must be anxious to get back to the hotel.' He eyed her blotchy face and still clutching fingers. 'A shower and a change of clothes would appear to be top priority.' For a second time he joined forces with Mahmoud. There was a rapid exchange of dialogue, then the servant nodded and set off back towards the beach. Jassim handed over Clemence's sandals. 'You'd better put these on,' he grinned, 'before there's another assassination attempt.'

Clemence bent, but as she did there came a tearing sound and the seam ripped further. With a yelp of exasperation, she grabbed for decency.

'Seems it's time for my Prince Charming act,' Jassim remarked, and gave a mock bow. 'Kindly allow me to fasten your glass slippers.'

Given any alternative, she would have rejected his droll offer of help. As it was she stood, first on one leg and then on the other, holding on to his shoulder all the while and clutching her torn catsuit.

'Thanks,' she managed to say, when he straightened.

'My pleasure, and now——' Jassim swept a gracious arm '—your carriage awaits.'

Her carriage turned out be a jeep, one which matched its owner in that the vehicle which had blocked her escape was battered, rusty and incredibly tough-looking. The windscreen was chipped in one corner and the number-plate tied on with wire. Presumably canvas existed somewhere to form a roof, but tonight the theme was fresh air.

Jassim flung her a doubtful look. 'We'd better cover you up,' he decided. 'The way you're dressed is enough to give a eunuch blood pressure!' He delved into the back of the jeep and after a moment of rummaging around triumphantly produced an old corduroy jacket. 'You can wear this. You'll sweat, but that can't be helped. I'd rather you didn't get yourself arrested.' A brow lifted. 'At least, not while I'm with you.' He waited until she had pulled on the jacket, then thwacked a hand across her buttocks. 'Let's go.'

This easy familiarity sparked off an identity crisis. Who was he—friend or foe? She wished she knew. Five minutes ago he had been scathing, now he was bewitching her with his smile. She felt like begging for the real Jassim Al Fori to please stand up. When he was domineering, he seemed every inch the hard man of the desert. Yet when he was relaxed, his casual, jokey Australian side came to the fore. Clemence accepted that was too simplistic, but it was how he appeared.

'Have you spent much time in Australia?' she asked.

'Thirty years. I was born and brought up there. I'm half Omani, yet it was only two years ago that I first set foot in the country. There was a lot of opposition, family stuff. Hop in,' he said, jerking a thumb.

Earlier she had been told to 'jump' into a low-level sports car, now she was expected to 'hop' into a high-stepped jeep. Clemence was pondering over the best way to climb aboard without further damage to both her catsuit and her reputation, when Jassim groaned.

'God Almighty!' He grabbed hold and dumped her in the passenger seat with as much regard as if she were a sack of coal. 'Shh.' An index finger was raised to block any complaints. Jumping in alongside, he swivelled and peered into the black depths of the gorge. 'Reversing out of here'll be like reversing blindfold, so I'd be grateful if you'd allow me to tackle the job without interruptions. OK?'

'OK.'

Jassim threw her a grin. 'Don't give way to the sulks.'

'I'm not, but there's no need for you to be so . . . bossy!'

'No?' He started the engine. 'It seems to me it's a bloody good job I am around to take charge. How else would you have coped?'

'For a start, if this decrepit heap of metal hadn't been in my way I'd have driven back to the main road,' said Clemence, with spirit.

'And then?'

'I'd have found my way back to the hotel.'

'In the dark? I doubt it.'

'Do you? Well, let me tell you something, I——'

'Shh!' The blocking index finger was raised again.

Mouth buttoned in seething mutiny, Clemence gathered the brown corduroy jacket around her. Several sizes too big, the shoulders hung halfway down her arms, but at least it made her respectable.

In reverse, they set off, bouncing up and down until her backside tingled from contact with the flat board seat. The jeep was short on frills, and although a belt was provided to keep her from being thrown out, she needed to grab for support wherever she could.

'I feel like I've gone a full ten minutes on a mechanical bull,' she sighed, when the perpendicular basalt walls gave way to open ground. 'It's a wonder I didn't——'

'No interruptions,' Jassim rapped, his fist clasping around the gear stick and plunging it into forward. He turned the jeep around. 'We're not clear yet. Once we hit the road you can gabble away all you like. Until then— silence.'

'Please,' she added sourly.

He grinned. 'Please.'

The speed of her incoming journey had allowed no opportunity to take stock, and now it came as a shock to realise how much of a death-trap lay between the gorge and the metalled highway. Pitfalls lurked everywhere, for the floor of the *wadi* was festooned with boulders, patches of soft sand, inexplicably sharp hillocks. Despite Jassim's careful control, twice they rocked alarmingly, and Clemence went cold remembering Khalid's reckless driving. The youth could have killed them both. Only providence had provided a safe path, as providence had provided Jassim. Providence? Clemence's heartbeat faltered. Her breath stopped. He had been in exactly the right place at the right time. That was too much of a long shot for providence.

Her thoughts ran amok. Why had he driven down to the beach? What part did he play? It had to be either good or bad; a man like Jassim Al Fori would not know how to be indifferent. She sneaked a suspicious sidelong glance. How could someone appear to offer solid gold security yet be a threat, at one and the same time? Trusting him—the white hunter—had been a grave error of judgement. Wasn't he

Khalid's brother? Same father, same genes, same devious desires. Clemence pulled the jacket closer. Where he fitted in was uncertain, but Jassim had to be involved in what had happened this evening, right up to his tanned neck. And to think she had fallen into his arms jabbering her gratitude like a maniac! Maybe he and Khalid had evolved a plan whereby one of them captured her, come what may? And tonight Jassim's luck was in.

Telling herself she must keep cool under crisis, Clemence thought hard. Earlier she had outmanoeuvred two people, why couldn't she outmaneouvre a third? By the time they reached the highway, another escape plan was being plotted. She would wait until they reached a traffic island and, as their speed slowed, jump out. Jassim would be caught unawares, and before he had time to react she would flag down a car. Clemence sucked in her lower lip. If she did jump out, the odds were she would crash to the ground. And if she didn't break every bone in her body, she might well be flattened by whatever vehicles were following behind.

She sneaked another look at the man beside her. Was he a threat? Her opinion of him fluctuated by the minute, no doubt because this evening her emotions had been put through the shredder. Jassim had sounded sincere when he had spoken of taking her back to the hotel, so why not sit tight, shut up, and hope for the best? Was there any other choice?

'No gabbles?' he enquired, when the miles were rolling by and Clemence remained mute. 'You're not suffering from delayed shock or something? You do feel all right?'

'Just a bit weary,' she said, with a fleeting smile.

'Care for a drink? Maybe it'd help revive you.'

She ran her fingers across a brow which burned and was sleeked with sweat. All of her burned and felt sweaty. The temperature inside the jacket equalled that of a sauna, and inside the catsuit it must be even higher. A drink seemed heaven-sent. On the point of accepting, Clemence hesitated. Was the offer some fiendish way of plying her with alcohol? After Khalid's performance down on the beach, nothing seemed too outlandish.

'What kind of a drink?' she questioned cautiously.

'I'm fresh out of Strawberry Daiquiris and Moscow Mules. Can't even rustle up the odd tube.' He jerked his head towards the rear of the jeep. 'All I have in there is water. I carry a few bottles in a coolbox as an emergency measure for if I should break down in the desert.'

'Water would be great.'

He swung off the highway, stopping on the sandy verge. A trip to the rear and Jassim was back, unscrewing the cap on a plastic bottle already beaded with condensation. He passed it to her, his smile full of encouragement.

Tipping back her head, Clemence swallowed. She gulped down several mouthfuls. 'Phew!' she exclaimed, wiping a trickle from her chin, and started to gulp again.

'Tastes good?'

'Better than champagne.'

In watching her, Jassim's dimple seemed to have become a permanent fixture. It was the kind of dimple which cried out for a finger to be traced down it, or to be gently kissed. Clemence gave herself a mental shake. Whatever was she thinking about? Dimple or no dimple, she must be circumspect in her dealings with this man. She had yet to discover whether or not he could be trusted, and disregarded the fact that he might be a villain at her peril. Thirst quenched, she handed back the water and was alarmed when, without bothering to wipe the neck, he promptly took his fill. Somehow the bottle passing straight from her lips to his seemed as intimate as if they had shared a toothbrush, and her image of him became even more confused.

'Feeling better?' asked Jassim, packing the water away.
'Much, thanks.'

When he resumed his seat beside her, she experienced an
odd sensation. It was as if the two of them had been sealed
off from the rest of the world, inside a glass bubble.
Intermittent traffic passed by on the road, yet it didn't
disturb them. A plane flew overhead, but neither of them
noticed. Jassim was still smiling, pleased with her recovery,
and she was drowning in that smile. The mosquito which
had buzzed around when he had kissed her was buzzing
again.

'Clemence,' he said, his voice and his eyes hesitant, 'isn't
it time you told me the real reason why your husband left
here in such a hurry?'

Splash! His question acted like a dash of the cold water
she had just drunk.

'You never let up, do you?' she accused. 'You heard what
Howard said. He went to see his mother.'

Jassim sighed. 'You know, I could easily fall for you. You
look beautiful, you play the harp beautifully.' He rammed
the jeep into gear and they swept back on to the road.
'Trouble is, I strongly suspect you tell lies beautifully, too.'

'How about me also being beautifully married?' she
retorted, riled at the way he had cut her off at the kneecaps.

'You don't *seem* married.'

'How many of us are what we seem?' Clemence
muttered, deciding that as enigmas went, Jassim Al Fori
had to be one of the greatest. Fighting stances had been
taken up again, and that suited her fine. She had plenty of
ammunition in store, why not use it? She surveyed her
target—the dark tousled head, aquiline nose, blunt jaw—
and lined up her first shot. 'Could you give me a straight
answer to a straight question?' she demanded. 'Could you
explain how you came to be driving to that particular
beach at that particular time, earlier this evening?'

He frowned at the road ahead. 'Chance. I sometimes go there for a swim and——'

'Who's lying beautifully now?' Clemence derided. 'I find it incredible how you managed to whizz up in the nick of time.'

'Talking about time, it's long after ten,' Jassim said, glancing at the watch strapped to his broad, hair-sprinkled wrist. 'How I came to be at the beach is unimportant. You weren't hurt. Khalid's learned his lesson. All I'm interested in is dropping you off at the Plaza and going home. It's been a long day.'

'As you're proving so evasive, I'll give myself a straight answer to that straight question,' she declared, her lip twisting. 'The reason you were on hand is that somehow you're tied into Khalid's sordid little seduction scene. It was a conspiracy!'

'No.' Jassim shook his head and sighed. 'I picked up a few clues and decided I'd better follow the pair of you, that's all.' He gave another sigh—longer, troubled. 'Up until that point I'd just been—suspicious.'

'Suspicious! But why? What have I ever done to——' Clemence read something in his profile. 'You were suspicious of Khalid, that's it, isn't it? That's why you've been turning up at the hotel day after day. You pretended it was me you didn't trust, but in fact it was your worm of a brother!' Jassim started to speak, but her anger had revved and now it kept going like a juggernaut out of control. 'You knew he had something planned, that he intended to lure me away to a desolate spot, and yet you stood by and did sweet nothing.' She thumped an irate fist against his shoulder. 'You bastard!'

'God Almighty, stop it! You'll make us crash!'

Clemence undertook a furious folding of her arms, flapping surplus sleeve all over the place. The temperature inside the jacket was soaring again. She felt hot and sticky, and . . . betrayed.

'Khalid's despicable,' she muttered, 'but you're far worse. You stood on the sidelines like a voyeur, watching and waiting.'

'It wasn't like that,' Jassim said curtly.

'No? You're as guilty as if you'd taken me down to that beach and—and raped me yourself!'

He gave an impatient grunt. 'Khalid didn't rape you.'

'He would have if he could.'

He put out a hand as if to touch her arm, then decided against it. 'Sunshine, in this life you have to learn to roll with the punches. I realise you were frightened, but all that happened this evening was that Khalid got fresh. OK, it was regrettable, but the kid's young and green. He has yet to learn how to sum up a situation and behave accordingly. I'm sure once he'd realised you genuinely found his attentions repulsive he'd have——'

Clemence did not allow him to continue. 'As you said a moment ago, it wasn't like that. He took me down to the beach with one aim in mind and *chuckled* when I said no!' She clasped her hands in her lap. 'Maybe I will report him to the police, after all.'

Jassim sighed. 'Have you any idea what would happen if you did? The rules here are far harsher than those in the Western world. If Khalid was found guilty of molesting you, chances are he'd be flogged, thrown into gaol and left to rot.'

'Serve him right!'

'You'd see his life ruined because of a boyish indiscretion?' He shook his head. 'I won't let you.'

'How do you propose to stop me?' she challenged.

The question was rhetorical, asked to prove her independence, nothing else. Regardless of Clemence's own need to avoid officialdom, she had no intention of reporting the matter to the police because, whatever she had said, doubts that Khalid would have forced her to do his bidding had begun to rise. It had only taken one pertinent knee to put a stop to his ideas. And sending the innocuous Mahmoud after her with her shoes scarcely seemed the act of someone hell-bent on ravishment. Until the episode at the beach, the youth had been polite and informative and had done his best to help. Had he really undergone a total change of character?

On consideration, she had to admit there could be faults on both sides, and maybe fifty-fifty. Bearing in mind that Khalid was immature and artless hadn't she, as *Mrs* Harrell, been a little too willing to befriend him? And being lonely and bored in a foreign country, maybe she had tended to hang on his every word? Who could blame him if he had misinterpreted her interest? The foreign factor might also have influenced her behaviour at the beach. Back home if a man had made a similar play for her, she would have slapped him down smartish and that would have been that. But she had been so entranced by the scene, she had allowed Khalid to gush compliments for what must have been minutes, with never a murmur. If the youth had been congratulating himself on the successful wooing of a compliant partner, couldn't it be construed as her fault? Clemence sighed. Yes. Which meant she would not be lodging any complaint because Khalid did not deserve it.

'One way to prevent any rash declarations would be to take you home with me for the night,' Jassim told her. 'Tomorrow, after a decent sleep, you'll see things in a different perspective. A sensible one.'

'Don't worry, I'm seeing things in a sensible perspective now,' she assured him, with a quick smile. 'Forget the police, I didn't mean it. Like you didn't mean it about taking me home.'

'Suppose I did?'

She glanced his way. 'A lone bachelor playing host to a married woman? Considering how strict the rules appear to be here, only a fool would live so dangerously.'

'But if the house was out in the wilds—which mine is— who's to know you were there? It would need you to broadcast the news—or me,' Jassim added significantly.

Clemence frowned. 'What point would there be in your telling anyone?' she enquired.

His reply was a shrug and raised eyebrows.

At the next roundabout, he swung the jeep left. They passed through a silent village, then motored up a long incline which brought them on to a flat, barren plain. No signs of life were visible. All she saw was a vast shadowy panorama of hard-packed sand, with the occasional stub of a tree appearing in the darkness. Monoliths of mountains rose in the distance, their peaks outlined in silver by the crescent moon.

'Have we turned inland?' she enquired, knowing she had not travelled this route with Khalid. He nodded. 'But the Plaza's on the coast.' He nodded again. 'Then why are we on this road?'

Jassim reduced their speed, and began to speak. 'Clem, a night at my house would do you no harm, and it could do me one helluva lot of good. You see, living here in Oman I'm a bit starved of girlfriends, so to speak, and——'

'Oh no!' Clemence's world crumbled. Just when she had been deciding he was a 'goodie', it came as a bitter blow to discover Jassim had been a 'baddie' all along. 'So now it's your turn to whip me off to some hideaway?' she demanded.

'Don't go overboard. I'm not "whipping" you off anywhere. All I'm suggesting is——'

'You don't want to sleep with me?' she jibed astringently.

'The honest answer to that would be—yes, I do. *But*,' he cautioned, raising a hand, 'I won't. You happen to be another man's wife and thus out of my territory. The law decrees so, likewise my mother. She brought me up to have morals and eat my greens, which means you can trust me.'

'Can I?'

'Cross my heart and hope to die,' vowed Jassim, making the necessary gestures. 'The only reason I'm suggesting you stay the night is that it's just struck me that your presence could be the solution to a long-term problem of mine. I'd be grateful for your co-operation.'

Clemence eyed him with suspicion. 'What happens if I refuse?' she enquired. 'What happens if——'

'Look at it this way, you'd be doing your good deed for the day.' She said two words which made him tut-tut. 'I didn't think nice girls knew words like that!'

'And I didn't think you thought I was a nice girl,' she retorted. 'Why should I do a good deed for someone who's accused me of every diabolical ploy under the sun?'

For a moment, a short one, he had the grace to look shamefaced. 'We got off on the wrong foot. My fault mostly, I admit, though you——'

'Me?' demanded Clemence.

'Forget it. No, there's no reason why you should do me a good deed. Unless, out of the kindness of your heart, you feel you could take pity on a fellow human being?'

'You're saying I should co-operate on humanitarian grounds?'

'That's one reason, and I'm doing my damnedest to line up others. Hell, if you're going to play hard to get I'm entitled to pull out all the stops to try and persuade you.' He grinned at her as though she were his favourite kind of candy. 'I should warn you I'm quite good at persuasion.'

Jassim's persuasion would be the kind that battered down brick walls, she thought, as he repositioned his grip on the steering-wheel, pushed his foot down on the accelerator, and continued to head inland.

'You'd be doing me a great favour,' he coaxed.

'I bet!'

'Clem, I'll fill you in on the details when we get there, but in the meantime trust me when I say I'm not about to violate you.'

Clemence was not sure. He sounded plausible enough, and yet ... Play it nice, play it cool, then pounce! Wasn't that the Al Fori way? This affable talk of a problem he would like her to solve *please* could be as tainted as Khalid's invitation to the barbecue. She held on tighter to her seat-belt. The mountains were closer now, gloomier and more forbidding. What lay beyond them? Jassim reckoned he was taking her to his house, but for all she knew he could be delivering her to the tribes in the interior as a foreign fillip for their slave-market.

'I don't want to know about your problem and I don't want to go to any house,' she declared. 'I just want——'

'Sunshine, we're nearly there, and it's a long haul back to the Plaza. Doing a U-turn at this late stage doesn't make much sense.'

To Clemence it made all the sense in the world. She would have told him so, but suddenly arguing seemed a waste of time. She had argued with Khalid, and where had that got her? And his brother was made of far sterner stuff. Once Jassim had chosen his path, she suspected it needed bombs, not arguments, to divert him. Well, she didn't have a bomb, but she could take action.

The traffic was spasmodic, but when the next headlights gleamed why not try to attract the driver's attention? The road ahead remained black and silent. Please let there be another car, Clemence appealed to the stars twinkling high above. It must have been five minutes later before pinpricks of light shone in the distance. Her heart cheered. Surreptitiously she eased open her seat-belt buckle The lights came nearer and nearer. Clemence lurched to her feet, unsteady in the stiletto-heeled sandals. One hand pawed for the support of the windscreen, the other was raised, ready to wave her frantic message.

Jassim glanced up in astonishment. 'What the hell?' he demanded.

She waved, she shouted, she swayed—swayed into him as her heel skidded beneath her. In reflex, he ducked and the jeep left the highway to rampage across the sand. Clemence's grip on the windscreen broke. She staggered in the moving vehicle, arms flailing for means of support. She found nothing. Her legs went from under her and she toppled out on to the Omani desert.

CHAPTER FIVE

CLEMENCE awoke with a start. Where was she? What had happened? All she knew was that she had slept like a stone. She stretched, then groaned. Stretching was agony. She also felt like a stone. The bed she lay on could not have helped, it had as much elasticity as a sacrificial slab. Turning her head to avoid a shaft of sunlight peeping in through a chink in hyacinth-blue curtains, she realised she was in a small bare room. Not a hospital, for the bed-linen was patterned in chic blue and white diagonals, and although the room held just one item of furniture, that item was an antique brassbound chest.

She lay still, trying to piece together the events which had brought her here. The memory of staggering to her feet in the jeep was clear, likewise her tumble, but after that everything blurred. She had a vague recollection of a bright light being shone into her eyes, and—what else? The smell of antiseptic, low rumbling voices, a sharp pain in her upper arm; had they been real or a dream?

Clemence raised a hand to rub her eyes and did a double take. Neat layers of white bandage were wound around her wrist and palm, the fingers protruding. Tentatively, she wiggled them. They felt stiff and sore, but no bones appeared to have been broken. She checked further and discovered, with relief, that the rest of her was undamaged, though aching like mad. Inch by torturous inch, she eased herself up on to the pillow, and received another surprise. She was wearing a man's shirt, a white silk shirt, an expensive white silk shirt, judging from the sensuous glide of the material across her skin. Did the shirt belong to Jassim?

Jassim! What had happened to him when they had careered off the road? Faces had swum into and out of her consciousness last night, but she had been too woozy to distinguish one from another. Had Jassim's been among them, or had he also been injured when the jeep had gone out of control? Visualising him pinned beneath a ton weight of rusty metal with his lifeblood draining away, Clemence felt haggard. If he had been hurt, it was her fault. She thought again. No, *his* fault. Considering how he had been driving her off somewhere against her will, she had been entitled to attempt to extricate herself. If he had suffered in consequence—tough luck! Her heart quaked. But dead? Jassim was never dead. His breed were survivors.

Hobbling across to the window, she pulled back the curtains. In horror, she gazed out at the miles and miles of flat sandy plain which wobbled and shifted in the heat. He had said his house was out in the wilds—it was, and then some. Indeed, Jassim might as well have rocketed her off to the moon. Jassim. Morosely she moved a toe along the tufts of the oriental rug, as fears for his safety sneaked back.

A tap on the door revived her. 'Come in,' she said hopefully, but her visitor turned out to be a skinny, dark-complexioned youth in an apple-green tunic and loose trousers. 'Where's Mr Al Fori? Is he safe?' Clemence enquired. The youth frowned. 'Has he been injured? Can I see him?'

His reply was a bob of the head and a gesture for her to follow him out on to a narrow whitewashed corridor. Five yards along, and the youth stopped outside a closed door. When he demonstrated with his hand that she was to enter, Clemence took a deep breath. What was she about to find— a broken man? On shaky legs, she stepped forward. She looked around. He had brought her to a bathroom! In protest, she turned, but the youth had vanished. Where was Jassim?

In an abrupt about-face she told herself to forget him. Why waste time worrying over someone who could be said to have condoned his brother's skulduggery, then insisted on passing off the incident as trivial, and who finally had had the effrontery to abduct her? Her first, her only thought, must be her own safety. Yet in the clear light of what she took to be morning, that safety did not appear to be so much in doubt. Last night her experience at the beach had left her shocked and emotional, not the best breeder for cool thought. Add to that a feeling of strangeness at being on the loose in Oman, and her apprehension at being driven away in the jeep had been dramatised out of all proportion. Now she was calm. Impending doom no longer appeared to be lurking just around the corner.

Having been provided with washing facilities, it seemed sensible to take advantage. She felt tacky. Sand was sticking to her skin, and a combination of stage make-up and last night's tears must mean her face looked a fright. A mirror would reveal the worst, but she could not find one. Like the bedroom, the bathroom was basic. Tiled in white, it possessed the spartan anonymity of a mortuary. There were no curtains at the opaque windows, no shelves bearing toiletries, no bath mats, not even, she saw, a lock on the door. Too bad. By now Clemence was determined to shower.

Fumbling with her left hand, she shucked off the shirt and stepped into the cubicle. A worn chromium lever controlled the spray, but at full volume all she achieved was a half-hearted trickle. Taking a shower in a trickle of water while holding her bandage clear required a variety of contortions. Before long Clemence was muttering. With wistful affection she recalled the refinements of the Plaza's guest bungalow—the high-pressure shower, the illuminated full-length mirrors, the well-sprung bed. Jassim must have his reasons for coming to the Middle East, but his Australian lifestyle had to have been on a loftier level than this—didn't it? She turned off the water and reached for a towel. Maybe not. Maybe if he was the poor relation here, he had been even poorer there?

Drying herself and easing back into the shirt demanded more indiarubber manipulations. By the time she had dressed, Clemence was weary. Rattled, too. Valiant attempts at fingercombing had not worked; her hair felt like a bird's nest. And despite repeated towelling her skin stayed damp. As a result, the semi-sheer shirt had moulded itself to her body, with an emphasis on her breasts. This was disturbing enough, but add her lack of underwear and she felt the unabridged version of a popsy pin-up—provocative, wanton and alarmingly physical. Her lips jammed together as she emerged into the corridor. Jassim Al Fori was responsible for this state of affairs. What a fitting judgement it would be if, at this very moment, he was lying in a hospital bed somewhere, encased in plaster from head to foot.

The sound of him laughing told her he was not. Clemence turned a corner, passed through an arch, and came upon him sitting at a dining-table, grinning up at the dark-skinned youth. A joke must have been shared, for Jassim's eyes were crinkled with amusement and his mouth curved enticingly. She subjected him to a swift inspection, but not a scratch nor a bruise was to be seen. He looked as healthy as a decathlon athlete, primed to break all records. Clemence did not know whether to feel relieved or infuriated.

He glanced up and smiled, then rose to his feet. As if unable to help themselves, his eyes began to move over her. Tinglingly aware of the picture she must present, she heard the buzz of the mosquito. That damned mosquito!

'What time is it?' Clemence asked, needing to break the silence. 'I appear to have mislaid my watch.'

Jassim pulled his eyes back to her face. 'Midday, and your watch is safe. How are you feeling?' he enquired, clicking into the role of concerned host.

'Stiff.'

'But not too ropey?'

'No,' she admitted.

He grinned, and said a few words of Arabic to the youth. 'I'm reassuring Sunthi—he's been worried about you. He's my houseboy. Let me introduce you.' There was more Arabic, and when the youth nodded, Clemence smiled a greeting. 'He comes from Pakistan, so his English is minimal. In comparison, Khalid's as fluent as an Oxford don.' Jassim pulled out a chair. 'Sit down, you must be famished. I was about to have scrambled eggs and tomatoes. Will that suit?'

Clemence hesitated. His manner was easy. Impending doom retreated even further, but couldn't joining him at the table be interpreted as an act of submission? Shouldn't she stand firm, castigate him for the rogue he was, and demand to be driven back to the hotel straight away? An aroma of freshly brewed coffee made her decide the journey could wait.

'Scrambled eggs sounds fine,' she agreed, sitting down.

Jassim sent Sunthi off into the kitchen, then reached for the percolator. 'Will you have a cup? Do you take milk? There's only goat's milk, but it tastes OK. Sugar?'

'Both,' said Clemence, and became busy, making desperate attempts to rearrange the shirt in such a way it provided the coverage of a blanket. The silk might envelop, but judging from how Jassim's eyes had been drawn down to her breasts, it seemed to be getting sheerer by the minute.

He suspended the milk jug above her cup. '*Please,*' he said, with a grin.

'Please,' she mumbled. 'I could have done that myself,' she protested, when Jassim added the sugar and began stirring her coffee.

'You'd deprive me of a chance to come good? Sunshine, with you incapacitated lending a hand is the least I can do. A slice of toast while you're waiting?'

'Yes. Please,' Clemence added.

'Butter?'

'Please.'

'Marmalade?'

'Yes. *Please*,' she said when he waited, and his grin spread.

Clemence was conscious of being drawn into a game, the kind of lighthearted, silly kind of game lovers play. One of her sleeves, pushed up to her elbow, had sagged and as he attended to her toast, she became frantic trying to fix it. They were not lovers. They were not even friends. And the sooner she returned to civilisation, the better.

'May I help?' asked Jassim, and leaned across the table to begin rolling the sleeve back into position.

At the touch of his fingers, Clemence froze. The action was too intimate. The way he had taken over the coffee-pouring and toast-preparation did nothing for her peace of mind, either. She waited, praying, praying he would leave her alone. And when he did, she was relieved—but itchy. She found herself wishing that today, instead of looking excessively *wholesome* in a fresh shirt and jeans, and with his jaw once again clean-shaven, Jassim would revert to being unkempt and mean. Then she would have known better how to cope with him.

'You've kidnapped me,' she accused, needing to insert a wedge between them.

'Kidnap is a very dirty word,' he rebuked. 'All I've done is keep you in protective custody overnight. You've been perfectly safe.'

She thrust her bandaged hand beneath his nose.

'Safe?' she demanded.

'Clem, if you will go throwing yourself from moving vehicles——' His shrug said the rest.

'I did not throw myself out. You were kidnapping me, and when I tried to escape you——'

'I what?' he enquired, when she dried up. 'I deliberately tipped you out? I deliberately drove the jeep off the road so that it sank up to the axles in soft sand? Have you any idea of the trouble you caused? I damn near developed a hernia attempting to push us free, just because I needed to take *you* to a doctor.'

'And did you?'

'Develop a hernia? Time alone will tell.' Jassim was curt. Presumably joking, but curt. He set the plate of toast before her. 'Regarding a doctor—yes, I did get you to one eventually. The diagnosis was that you were suffering from concussion. Thank God!'

'I appreciate your concern.'

'Clemence, when I saw you lying on the sand I imagined crushed ribs, internal bleeding, a coma, the lot,' he told her, his curtness shifting into anger. 'Mere concussion came as a blessed relief. The doctor gave you a sedative and reckoned you'd feel fine when you woke up. You've told me that you do.'

'No, I said I didn't feel too ropey.'

'If I had a rope here right now, I'd be tempted to string you up from the nearest tree,' Jassim declared. 'What the hell were you playing at last night? When I have a woman driving with me she usually wants to snuggle closer, not take damn pratfalls!'

'I didn't intend to fall, I intended to—to make a bid for freedom!' Clemence retorted, and scowled when his laughter told her she had sounded melodramatic.

'You didn't need to go to those lengths. I would have listened to reason.'

'I asked to be taken back to the hotel, and you said no U-turns.'

Jassim had a mouthful of coffee. 'I also assured you you'd come to no harm and promised to explain all when we arrived here.'

'You were imposing your will,' she declared, finding it hard to admit she had panicked in what now seemed a supremely daffy kind of way. 'Howard's great at ordering me to do this, do that, but you're ten times worse. I'd get out of ready-mixed concrete and join the Army, if I were you. Your natural role in life is a sergeant-major!'

'Maybe I did overrule you,' he said, in a thoughtful admission of error.

'There's no maybe about it.'

'But jumping to your feet in a speeding jeep has to be marked down as one of the stupidest, most reckless events of the year. You have a kamikaze streak, y'know that?'

Clemence's patience snapped. 'OK, I was too impulsive,' she flung at him.

'You were.'

'And who's to blame?' She raised her bandaged hand. 'This would never have happened if you hadn't—oh no!' she exclaimed. 'How am I going to play my harp?'

Sunthi appeared at that moment, bearing the scrambled eggs, and there was a pause as he set the plates down and retreated, smiling.

'Your wrist'll only be out of action for three or four days at most,' Jassim told her. 'You were complaining about it aching last night, so I had the doctor take a look. He thinks your arm must have been wrenched when you did your free-fall act. However, he assured me nothing was torn.' He gestured towards the steaming plate. 'Shall I feed you?'

'I can manage, thanks,' she said, and began left-handedly shovelling scrambled egg into her mouth at top speed.

One way and another Jassim had done more than his

quota of helping. Even if her plight could be attributed to him, his subsequent behaviour had been beyond reproach. Part of her wanted to thank him, part of her was tempted to apologise, yet part of her insisted everything must be laid at his door. If Jassim had not shanghaied her, none of this would have happened.

'While I was out for the count, you appear to have been busy,' Clemence remarked, her tone edging dangerously close to gratitude. 'What time did we end up here?'

'Near enough to two a.m.'

She frowned, feeling guilty, then gave a chirpy smile. 'Well, at least you've been able to sleep late this morning.'

'No chance. I was up at dawn.' He bit into a slice of toast. 'I needed to report into the depot to warn them they'd have to do without me for a while. There's no phone here, so going in person was the only way.'

'Your boss didn't mind?'

'My boss?' Jassim grinned. 'No, he's the understanding type.' He chewed on the toast. 'And after calling at the depot, I went on to the Plaza.'

'Why?'

'Sunshine, you waltzing around in a filmy shirt might appeal to you as much as it appeals to me.' For a moment the green eyes were naughty, then he called himself to heel. 'But I consider it my duty to protect Sunthi from——' his eyes became naughty again. 'What shall I say?'

'Nothing.'

He laughed. 'I went to your bungalow and collected what I hope are sufficient clothes to see you through the next few days.'

Clemence put down her fork. 'The next *few* days?'

'As you can't play your harp, you might as well stay here.'

'No, thanks!'

'But you arriving back at the hotel like a wounded

soldier will give the wrong impression.'

'Hard luck!' snapped Clemence, then relented. 'Jassim——'

'Jass.'

'Jass, if you're worried about me spreading tales to the effect you were responsible for my injury, don't be. Although you were hijacking me, I was the one who stood up in the jeep, so I'm the one to blame,' she conceded.

'You've got it all wrong. Yes, the jeep business was your fault,' he agreed, far more energetically than she felt was necessary. 'But what matters is that in order to solve the problem I spoke of yesterday, I'd like to be able to imply that you and I have enjoyed a night, or nights, of——' he frowned '—unbridled passion. You with a bandaged hand tends to reduce the credibility.'

'Isn't it time you explained this problem?' Clemence asked, chasing a final nugget of scrambled egg around her plate.

He took the fork from her fingers. 'Open up,' he instructed, and popped the egg into her mouth. 'The problem is a woman. I appear to be blighted with troublesome females,' he remarked laconically. 'You see, when I first came to Oman I found myself up against a wall of aggression. My father's family had been furious when he'd got involved with my mother all those years ago, and——'

'He met her in Australia?'

'Yes, he went to study engineering. It's a long story,' he said dismissively. 'When I arrived here two years ago I went through a period of feeling isolated, and this woman stretched out a hand. I was grateful—bloody appreciative, in fact. From the start I regarded our interaction as platonic—any other kind of relationship never occurred to me—but wires must have got crossed because in time she began to act as if, although I wasn't paying court, I should.'

Jassim blew out his cheeks in bewilderment. 'She's a
goodlooker and plenty of men do get hooked, which is
maybe an added reason why she considers I ought to be
interested. About a month ago she dropped a very large
hint to the effect that we'd wasted enough time pussyfoot-
ing around and she was more than ready for something
serious. That laid me out flat. I decided there was no other
way than to tell her thanks, but no, thanks.'

'And?' asked Clemence.

'And I did.'

'And?'

'And the damn woman won't get the message. Trouble is
she's volatile and has been known to be vindictive, so I guess
I've been handling her with kid gloves.'

'You should be good at that.'

He acknowledged the dig with a rueful smile. 'I keep
slipping memorable clichés like "I'm not interested in a
commitment" into the conversation, but she persists with
the idea that sooner or later I'll want to settle down. I do,
but—God Almighty!—not with her. It doesn't help any
that ever since I've known her there's been a dearth of
females in my life. It's not by choice I live on the wrong side
of the monastery walls, and I have taken a couple of short
trips back to Brisbane when I've kicked up my feet, as
Khalid would say, but here I spend most of my time
working. And even if I had enough energy left at the end of
the daily ten-hour slog, where would I look for company?
Omani women are heavily chaperoned, while Western
girls are few and far between. More coffee?'

'Please. So you'd like to use me as a decoy?' Clemence
asked, as he filled her cup.

'If you're agreeable. I reckon evidence of another woman
in my life should make her back off. I guarantee you won't
be compromised. No way will I queer things for you with
Howard.'

'He won't mind,' she replied without thinking, and flushed. 'I mean——'

'I know what you mean.' Jassim paused. For a moment he seemed about to slew the conversation around, but for some reason changed his mind. 'No one apart from this one woman will be aware you've stayed here with me. For example, when I came across Otto at the hotel this morning, I——'

'Oh dear! He was supposed to be showing me the sights today,' she said, suddenly remembering.

Jassim nodded. 'He was looking for you. However, I told him I'd fixed you up on a desert safari with a couple of my friends and you'd left the hotel at daybreak.'

'He believed that?'

'Why not? Incidentally, don't worry about not being able to play your harp. The Indians' debut was a roaring success. They'll be back at the Plaza this evening.'

'You seem to have everything arranged,' Clemence said cryptically.

He grinned. 'My school-leaving report did make reference to my organisational skills.'

'Highly developed ones. You've taken control of me, lock, stock and barrel.' A thought hit her. 'Did you undress me?'

'Who else? But you can take that stricken look off your face. The catsuit was not only torn, but thick with sand, so putting you into something clean seemed the decent thing to do. *Decent*.' Jassim underlined the word. 'I peeled away the cloth of gold and covered you up in the shirt in, at most, two seconds flat. All that interested me in the early hours of this morning was crawling into bed and going to sleep— alone.'

'Where's my catsuit now?'

'At the hotel, being laundered and undergoing running

repairs.' He cocked a brow at her hair. 'As we've finished eating, how about you receiving running repairs with the aid of a comb?'

'Please.'

'So polite? Seems I could be training you,' he commented with amusement. 'Shall we go?'

Down the corridor he led her, and into his bedroom. Once again the décor was frugal—whitewashed walls, a pine bed, the minimum amount of furniture. For a man who spent most of his time working, Jassim had precious little to show for it in the way of possessions.

'Thanks,' she said, when he handed her a comb.

A shaving-mirror had been propped up on a chest of drawers, and Clemence moved back and forth seeking her reflection. Finding it, she began a lefthanded attempt to tame her corn-coloured tangle of damp hair. The task was not easy, and Jassim watching did not help. Once again there was too much intimacy around.

'Your parting's pathetic,' he grumbled, and turned her to face him.

Commandeering the comb and with the tip of his tongue protuding from between his teeth, he studied her. Whine, went the mosquito. He was close. So close. Only a few inches of air separated them. His fingers on her chin as he tilted her head rooted Clemence to the spot. There was a sombre look in his green eyes. He's going to kiss me, she thought, her heart racing, and knew this time she would never be strong enough to protest. Don't come any closer, she begged silently. Please do. But Jassim was merely organising her. With the precision of a draughtsman, he re-did her parting.

'There,' he said, when every single hair had been combed into place.

She inspected herself in the mirror. 'You've missed your vocation,' she told him.

If there was pique in her voice, he failed to hear it.

'I need to go into the depot now,' he said, becoming businesslike. 'I'll be away two or three hours, so why don't you take a siesta? That's what Sunthi does every afternoon. Your clothes are in your bedroom. I've also provided some books, and——'

'Hold on!' Clemence protested, annoyed to discover she was on the brink of being marooned. 'I haven't agreed to go along with this scheme of yours yet.'

'We'll discuss it later.'

'No. Now.'

Jassim flung her an impatient look. 'Don't give me the runaround, sunshine.'

'I'm not, but——'

'You didn't seem too anti earlier. What's happened, are you having second thoughts?'

'I'm not having any thoughts. That's the trouble. I need a little time to——'

'But I don't have time,' he said, looking at his watch. 'I promised the guys at the depot I'd be in early afternoon, and if I don't turn up soon they'll be sending out a posse.'

'I thought you had an understanding employer?' Clemence retaliated. 'Surely ten minutes——'

'It's important I go to work,' Jassim said through his teeth, and in one stride was at the door. 'While I'm away, be a good girl and think things over. OK?'

'No, it's not,' she started to say, but he had gone.

She heard him call out to Sunthi, then a distant door slammed. She sighed, and at the sound of a surging engine marched along the corridor and into the room where she had awakened. Sure enough her soft-top suitcase was sitting on the bed, her watch beside it. A quick check through proved Jassim had brought everything required for her stay, right down to shoulder-bag and pair of flat sandals. He had even brought her bikini. How organised, Clemence thought sourly, as she dressed herself in a long-sleeved café-au-lait blouse and trousers. She slid her feet into the sandals, then walked over to the window. Hands in her pockets, she stared out.

Why should she stick around just to suit him? she wondered, rankled at being so cursorily discarded. After all, she was supposed to be married. As *Mrs* Harrell would she have been willing to act as a decoy? It seemed doubtful. More likely a wife would have rejected his scheme outright. Clemence frowned. In retrospect it was strange how the married angle had been only a peripheral feature. Although she could have employed it to give clout to a refusal, she hadn't. As for Jassim—he acted almost as though it was taken for granted that the relationship between her and Howard had its limitations.

But Jassim Al Fori took too much for granted, she decided with a spasm of irritation. Like her remaining here where he had dumped her and being a good girl. A good girl—how chauvinistic! What gave him the right to order her around? If she wished to return to the hotel, then return to the hotel she would. A compulsion to demonstrate her independence had Clemence searching the view. Eyes narrowed, she studied the scene. The house was built on the edge of a plain, at the foot of bare hills which stretched back into mountains. Earlier it had seemed to exist in splendid isolation, but ... When she discovered a series of small white blobs tucked into the horizon, she smiled. The blobs had to be a village. A village meant a telephone, and a telephone meant she could ring the Al Fori Plaza and arrange for a taxi to collect her. What a shame she would miss Jassim's surprise and irritation, when he returned to discover the good little girl had bolted!

Departure decided, next Clemence planned for survival. The distance to those blobs must only be a mile or two, which eliminated any risk of being set upon by wandering

Bedouin, yet the burning sun could turn her walk into a
marathon unless she went prepared. In her shoulderbag
she located a pair of owl-type sunglasses. She put them to
one side, then went through to speak to Sunthi. With great
comic play, Clemence demonstrated how thirsty she felt.
Could she have some water—she pointed to a flask—for her
bedside? Grinning at her antics, the houseboy was pleased
to oblige. On her way back along the corridor, she sneaked
into Jassim's room and discovered that, in his rush to leave,
he had left his slouch hat on a hook behind the door. How
convenient! She lifted it down and sat it on her head. The
hat was on the large side, so her final coup was to purloin
two handkerchiefs and stuff them into the crown.

Back in her room, Clemence waited. Before long the
faint noises from the kitchen ceased and the house fell silent.
She made herself wait ten mintes, then tiptoed along the
corridor and across the dining-room. Earlier she had taken
note of a door, and now she cautiously opened it and went
out into a hallway. The front door was closed, but a key
protruded from the lock. Clemence bundled her hair on top
of her head and tugged on the slouch hat. Next the
sunglasses were put in place. Finally she gripped the water
flask in her left hand, and stepped out into the furnace
which was the afternoon.

The heat took her breath away. For a moment she
hesitated, recovering from the impact, then sallied forth. In
minutes she was wet. Sweat streamed down her face,
trickled between her shoulder blades, bobbled her breasts.
The glasses skated down her nose, and beneath the hat the
knot of hair became a sodden hank of gold. Clemence
trained her eyes on the white blobs, and walked and walked
and walked.

High above in the clear blue sky, a hawk glided on a
thermal, a dark ominous shape. No, not ominous. The bird
was not a vulture, biding time before it swooped to pick at

her flesh the moment heatstroke keeled her over. Clemence wiped a damp palm on her backside, pushed up the spectacles, and renewed her grip on the water flask. She must not drink anything yet, she had only been walking for fifteen mintues. Only fifteen? Fifteen parched minutes. Fifteen sweltering minutes. Fifteen uncomfortable minutes, for the stiffness in her bones which had receded seemed to have returned. She kept moving. The sun burned through the hat on her head, the sand burned through the sandals on her feet, her wrist bandage became a damp rag. The hawk continued to circle. She pulled the brim of the slouch hat down over her brow, and put one foot before the other.

Twice she stopped for a swig of water, and twice the white blobs remained white blobs, At one point she wondered if her eyes might be playing tricks. Forty minutes across the plain and her legs felt weak. Should she turn back? That mile or two had begun to seem a laughable assessment. Fifty minutes and the white blobs took shape. She was *not* turning back. The blobs crystallised into single-storey Middle Eastern houses, the inevitable square of the air-conditioner stamped mid-wall. Around the houses blackened *sumr* trees fought for survival, and beneath the trees were goats. As Clemence approached some wandered out to meet her, though the wiser ones remained in the shade. The houses, each equipped with a television aerial and washing on the roof, were silent. She saw not a single soul. But of course, it was siesta time.

A giggle had her spinning round. Pressed against a wall Clemence saw a tiny girl in bright blue cloth, with a silver flower screwed into one nostril. She was smiling, her kohl-rimmed eyes huge with curiosity. Clemence smiled back. She was about to mime her need of a telephone, when the child darted away. Seconds later a gang of children were eyeing her, some giggling, others solemn as judges. Clad in robes of red and purple and orange, they reminded her of a

cloud of butterflies. Older girls materialised, graceful doe-
eyed creatures swathed in white muslin, who whispered
together. Then a door opened, a woman peeped out. Robed
men began to appear, gazing gravely from beneath their
tasselled *shemags*. Siesta time or not, from every house at
least one person emerged to inspect the new arrival.

Clemence eased off the slouch hat and shook out her
damp locks. At a stroke the giggles and the whispering
ceased. Everyone stared. The silence was deafening. Even
the goats seemed to have paused mid-chew. I'm an alien,
she thought—not extra-terrestrial exactly, but near
enough. Then a child laughed and a murmur brushed the
crowd. Smiling, people pointed to her hair. A babble of
conversation started, and Clemence felt happier.

'Excuse me,' she said, heading for the nearest woman, but
the woman giggled and backed away. The second female
she tried also smiled and retreated. Clemence approached a
man. 'Telephone?' she enquired, dialling in mid-air. He
remained where he was, his expression as forthcoming as a
basilisk's. 'Does anyone understand English?' she appealed.

No answer. Jassim's house lacked a telephone and, it
seemed, so did the village. Civilisation had its limits. The
time had come for reappraisal, and so Clemence squinted
into the sunshine. Ahead lay a further expanse of sandy
plain and—yes, more white blobs. But the rebellion which
had insisted she do her own thing had faded. Forward
meant the unknown, backward meant Jassim—wasn't he
infinitely preferable? There were moments when she had
to admit she liked him. She frowned. Like was the wrong
word. The emotion he aroused was far stronger. Even if
sparks did tend to fly whenever they were together,
underlying it all was attraction with a capital A. They
spoke the same language, shared a sense of humour. And
what about that mosquito? Considering they had only
known each other a short time, a remarkable degree of

involvement existed. Clemence did not normally put much faith in instant rapport, but there was no denying her life had taken on a brilliant edge now she had discovered Jassim was around.

She rammed the slouch hat on her head, and was all set to retrace her steps when a cloud of dust appeared amidst the *sumr* trees. She waited. The entire village waited. The dust cloud came nearer, firming itself into a clapped-out old jeep driven by a dark-haired man in dusty clothes.

Trust Jassim to follow me! she thought, obliterating thoughts of how, a moment ago, she had planned to return. Glaring from beneath the brim of the too large hat, Clemence remained immobile as the jeep roared up beside her.

He cut the engine and jumped out. 'What do you think you're doing?' he demanded, his green eyes flashing. 'Taking part in a sponsored bloody walk?'

CHAPTER SIX

CLEMENCE's chin jutted. 'I left,' she informed him. 'I was fed up with being a good girl, fed up with toeing your line, fed up with being allowed no space in which to breathe, so I left.'

'Good on you, mate!' Jassim spoke in terse Australian tones. 'You upped and left, but what about everyone else? What about Sunthi? The lad's worried sick. He met me on the doorstep babbling about you falling into quicksands and never being seen again.'

'Quicksands in the desert?' The eyes behind the owl sunglasses became suddenly perturbed.

'There's an area called Umm as-Samim where entire herds of goats have been swallowed up, plus a camel or two.'

'And that's around here?'

'No,' he replied, as though he wished it were. 'Umm as-Samim lies to the east of the Empty Quarter, but Sunthi doesn't have much sense of geography. A safe route across is supposed to be known only to one tribe, the Duru. Duru men are tall and fierce and domineering. They roam the wilds of Oman like a pack of rapacious animals. Everyone needs to take care when they approach, and you——' Jassim jabbed a finger '—were lucky not to have come up against one.'

Clemence blessed him with what passed for a smile. 'I already have.'

'Oh no! The Duru might have all the time in the world to

98

spend racing around the desert in pursuit of crackpot females, I don't.'

'Why aren't you at work?' she demanded. 'You said you'd be gone two or three hours.'

'I finished early because, if you must know, I wanted to make amends. I felt bad about the things I said to you at the beach last night, and I felt guilty about leaving you on your own. But I needn't have bothered, need I?'

'I was coming back,' she said, his rebuke making her shuffle her feet and tighten her lefthanded grip on the water flask. 'And I'm sorry if Sunthi was worried.'

'You should be. He's taken quite a shine to you. Though if he could see you now he'd most certainly change his mind—if not fall about laughing.' A brow twitched. 'In my shirt you looked delightful. To be honest, when you walked in through the arch this morning all my fantasies were in danger of coming to life in one fell swoop, and I imagine Sunthi felt very much the same. However, in my hat—— Jassim's anger had faded and dry amusement had taken its place '—I swear if you didn't have ears it'd be sitting on your shoulders. The damp patches and sweaty face don't do much for the cause of glamour, either. You look like Clint Eastwood on a bad day.' He glanced around, seeming to notice the watching villagers for the first time. 'God knows what the folks here must have thought when you moseyed into town. You do realise you've ruined the reputation of the English Rose for all time?'

'Who says?' she challenged, and with a flourish took off the slouch hat.

Drier now that her trek had been halted, her hair fell to her shoulders. She moved her head and as her blonde mane rippled like ripe corn in the sunshine, the villagers, to the last child, gawked admiringly.

'Instant stardom,' commented Jassim, his dimple shining. One of the men called out and he answered in quick-fire Arabic. 'A simple translation would be that you're worth looking at.'

'Clint Eastwood on a bad day?'

He laughed. 'I take it all back.' Set to pat her rear end, he remembered their audience and instead gestured towards the jeep. 'We'll call in at the house and collect your clothes, then continue straight on to the hotel.' When he saw she was hesitating, he made a sweeping gesture. 'Come *on!*'

Clemence did as she was told and climbed in beside him. Now that the afternoon's entertainment had ended, the villagers began to disperse. Only the children stayed, and they moved back as he gunned the engine.

'What makes you think I want to go to the Plaza right this minute?' she questioned, pulling down her dark glasses and looking at him over the top.

Jassim groaned. 'Sunshine, you've vaulted out of a jeep and set off on a route march, remember? Subtle actions like these do make me realise you possess a certain determination to reach the hotel, come what may. Indeed, if we hang around here much longer it wouldn't surprise me if you started to levitate.'

She thrust the glasses back up her nose. 'You've realised damn all! Nothing I've said has got through to you, has it?'

'What are you talking about?' he enquired, with an air of flat resignation.

'Me deciding what *I* want to do!'

'This is a fight for autonomy?'

'No, it's simply a plea to be allowed to do things *my* way, once in a while.'

'OK, I give up. You win. What do you want to do?'

'You're giving me a choice?'

An arm ripped through the air in an extravagant gesture of masculine frustration. 'God Almighty!—yes.'

'In that case, I would like to go to your house, stay the three or four days required to bring my wrist back to full strength, and then return to the hotel,' Clemence said quietly.

'Why the change of heart?'

'Isn't it permitted?' she countered.

'Sunshine, who am I to stand in your way?'

'In addition, I agree to acting as a decoy in order to try and rid you of your pestering lady-friend. Incidentally, what's her name?'

'Let's just call her Mrs X,' he said tersely, and his hand moved on the gear stick.

'Mrs?'

'She's a widow.'

'Would you like your hat?' Clemence offered, when they were driving along.

'Keep it. The sun's still fierce.' Jassim frowned out at the track of hard-packed sand which lay ahead. 'I said I felt bad about last night and I do, but it's not just those remarks I regret. All along I've been rough on you. Behaved like a true blue bastard, in fact. I don't suppose there's a chance you could forgive me?'

'It might be possible.'

'I apologise. Sincerely. Most sincerely. From the bottom of my heart.'

Clemence smiled at his hangdog expression. 'Very nicely said.'

'I mean it.' He threw her a quick look. 'I'm fresh out of sackcloth and ashes, but would it help any if I stopped the jeep and prostrated myself on the sand?'

'Hands and knees will do.'

'Whatever you say,' he grinned, and braked.

'Not really,' she protested, stricken by the idea that he might leap out and drop to all fours. He laughed, and they picked up speed again. 'So you accept my character is spotless?' Clemence asked, feeling an intense spurt of satisfaction. Being in his good books was far superior to being in his bad.

He nodded. 'I should have known that all along, but it was difficult to reconcile——' He stopped speaking and started again. 'By way of mitigating circumstances I ought to explain that past events, in the form of two prime examples of the mercenary female, have made me somewhat jaundiced.'

'And having met two, you were on the look-out for a third?'

''Fraid so. However, this morning Khalid gave a detailed account of what had happened and accepted full responsibility.'

'That's not quite fair,' she protested.

'It is,' Jassim said heavily.

'No, he wasn't entirely to blame. I think, under the circumstances, I could have been a bit too ... friendly,' Clemence explained. 'Combine that with Howard giving the wrong idea by magnanimously informing him he could do with me as he wished, and was it Khalid's fault if——'

'It *was* Khalid's fault,' he insisted.

She shrugged, then tipped her head to one side and grinned mischievously. 'You say he *gave* an explanation? You're sure you didn't take him out into the desert and tie him to a stake?'

'No need. Leyla unexpectedly arrived back last night from Paris.' Jassim grimaced. 'Maybe at times I come on too strong, but you should see her in action. She might dote on her son, but when she took control of extracting a confession she damn near extracted his toenails as well. By the time she'd finished, the kid was almost in tears and so was I. You know the song, "Whatever Lola wants, Lola gets"? Change the name to Leyla and you have her measure.' He shuddered with some private horror. 'She's always kept Khalid under her thumb, which is where she'd like to keep everybody, but this morning he was steamrollered, hammered and battened down.' He glanced across at Clemence and suddenly grinned. The jeep's movement had edged the slouch hat lower and lower until it was lodged on the top of her sunglasses. 'Eat your heart out, Clint Eastwood,' he recited.

In the shade of the brim, Clemence wrinkled her nose.

Her outward slog had taken well over an hour, but they arrived back at the house in less than fifteen minutes. The moment they drew under the corrugated-iron canopy which served as a garage, Sunthi ran out. A translation of the excited rush of his speech was unnecessary, relief at her safety showed in his wide smiles.

'I've explained that you'll be staying for a few days,' Jassim told her, when the houseboy had calmed down and they went indoors. 'Having a female on the premises is cause for celebration, you understand? So for dinner we shall be having one of Sunthi's "specials"—beef curry with chutney and sambals.'

'Sounds tasty.'

'It is. However, as it won't be ready for a while suppose we have a swim.'

Clemence recalled the miles and miles of hard-baked desert that stretched to the horizon.

'A swim sounds tasty too, but where?'

'In my pool.'

'You have a pool?'

He laughed at her astonishment. 'Put on your swim-ming-togs, and I'll show you.'

With a kanga tied over her white bikini, Clemence stepped out of her room five minutes later. Jassim was waiting. He wore brief black trunks and had a towel slung over one shoulder. Padding after him, she thought it was impossible not to notice how muscular he was. Notice and admire. His shoulders were broad, whittling down to a lean waist and what Yvonne had once praised in Howard—a neat seat. But unlike Howard, who tended to be lanky and lolloping, he moved with a supple grace. His skin was smooth and golden. He would be warm to touch, she thought, and without warning her fingertips tingled.

Jassim led her through the kitchen—tossing a joke at Sunthi in passing—and opened a door on to a small sunlit courtyard.

'The view from the front of the house might be sterile and monotonous, but it's different at the rear,' he said.

As Clemence lifted her eyes and looked beyond the low stone wall at the far end of the courtyard, she realised he was guilty of a classic understatement. Against the wall dwarf palms marked the beginning of a lush garden which stretched back to where the land rose up in the first beginnings of the mountain range. Here the hillside curved to make a natural amphitheatre. She stared at it in amazement. The rock which should have been bare and inhospitable sprouted glossy leaves from crevices, had hibiscus and oleander competing for space, grew flowers and feathery fronds everywhere. It was like coming across a quarter-acre of rampant jungle in the middle of the Sahara.

'Why?' she asked simply.

'Higher up in the mountains there's a spring which is fed

by the rain which falls further back in the range. The water irrigates the rock face and finishes up in a pool.'

Jassim allowed her a minute to stand and stare, then directed her through a gate at the far end of the courtyard and along a path between the stiff, bluish-green palms. Tropical vines and ivies besieged them on all sides, luxuriant lianas and orchids scented the air, ferny fronds brushed at their ankles. Clemence was so busy marvelling that they had reached the pool before she noticed. It was an oval pool, edged with emerald green mosses, and large enough and deep enough for proper swimming. If her wrist had not been bandaged, she would have been tempted to plunge in then and there. Instead it was Jassim who dived, while she walked round to find a shallower spot where she removed her kanga and sat on the edge.

'Want me to help you in?' he suggested, surfacing only a yard or two away from where she dangled her legs in the crystal-clear water. He jerked his head to flick the hair from his eyes, and behind him a shower of diamond drops scattered across the pool's surface. 'I'm afraid there's nothing so convenient as steps to enter by.'

'No, I'm OK,' Clemence assured him hastily. A few minutes ago she had needed to fight the temptation to touch him, yet now the idea of his touching her, even on a casual, helpful basis, took on a dangerous slant. 'I can slide in—like this!'

She landed in the water with more of a twist and a turn and a plop than a slide. But she did it alone. Her injured wrist held high like a mast, she managed one or two lengths of a somewhat lopsided breaststroke. After that she floated on her back, then doggy-paddled, but much as she enjoyed swimming in what had turned out to be surprisingly cool water, acting the one-handed mermaid was tiring. As

Jassim powered up and down in an easy crawl, she covertly examined the pool perimeter. Was there a place where she could climb out unaided? In the end Clemence had to admit defeat.

'Could you give me a hand, please?' she asked.

Jassim did so, literally. In one fluid movement, he swung himself from the water and on to the stone edge. He reached down. 'Hold on tight,' he instructed, linking strong brown fingers with hers. He gave one firm tug, which heaved her out of the pool and into his arms.

After that he should have released her, or Clemence should have stepped away, but neither of them moved. He was holding her close, so close her body throbbed with the nearness of his.

'Thanks,' she murmured. When Jassim smiled and the long dimple appeared, her hand rose as if by remote control. With the tip of her finger she stroked a slow path down the groove. His skin *was* warm and slippery wet. 'Smooth.' She drew the word out. 'Whatever happened to your five o'clock shadow?'

'I don't dare omit to shave, not now. Not after the way you looked at me.'

'How was that?'

'As though I was one of the great unwashed. Two years in the Omani outback and I'm turning primitive.' He rolled his eyes, then grew serious. 'Living a basic kind of life is probably the reason for my caveman tactics with you. Both last night, when I came up with the idea of your staying here, and today when I left to go to work, I admit I could be accused of laying down the law. I've become so used to giving orders to my underlings and expecting them to jump, it seems I've fouled up on my gentle touch.'

'You have underlings?'

'One or two.'

Clemence laughed. 'Sounds like I was lucky you didn't thump me on the head with a club last night and drag me here by the hair!'

'My social graces might have grown rusty, but not to the point that I've forgotten that that kind of behaviour is inadmissible,' he said, and frowned. His arms fell from her. He stepped back. 'With a married woman.'

'Oh,' she said, the supposed status taking her unawares.

Jassim gazed at her as if searching for hidden conversation in her eyes. 'I don't suppose there's anything you'd like to tell me?' he enquired.

'Such as?' she asked, playing for time.

Howard had warned against revelations, but should she confess she was a long way from married? The idea was tempting. The moment seemed right. Jassim's discretion was a prerequisite, but she trusted him not to go rushing to the authorities with a demand that they look closer into her file, so where was the harm in making him a confidant?

'Let's sit,' he suggested, and took hold of her hand to half coax, half propel her down beside him on the edge of the pool. Resting back on his arms, he stared down the length of his legs to where his feet were submerged. 'Clem, when I went to your bungalow to get your clothes I—I discovered something,' he said awkwardly.

'Oh!' she said again, but this time the exclamation had moved up a notch.

The only thing he could have discovered was that she was single. It must be. Agreed, she had been on the brink of telling him herself, but to find he already knew switched everything around. Clemence's mind buzzed. Access to that particular piece of information lay via her passport, which had been left in the top drawer of the desk. The drawer had been locked, but the key had been in her purse inside her shoulder bag. Her temper flared. Ye gods, Jassim must have been snooping, and with a vengeance! She slung a fierce look sideways. How dared he rifle through her belongings? Well, if he expected her to collapse in a heap when confronted with the fact she was not Howard's wife, he was mistaken. Maybe she had arrived in Oman illegally, but it was not through any flagrant deception on her part. The one at error had been Bernie.

Clemence sat as straight as a tin soldier. 'So?' she demanded.

'Sunshine, there's no need to go on the defensive with me.'

'I'm not. I have nothing to be defensive about. All that happened was that before we came to Oman, Howard——'

'Got himself another woman?'

She gave a startled laugh. 'How did you know?' she gasped, the breath knocked out of her by this unexpected assertion.

'She's the reason he returned home and left you here?'

'Yes, but——'

'I thought as much. His behaviour in Khalid's office was odd. He went on at great length about needing to be with his mother, but the story never rang true.'

Clemence bent her head. 'It was the only excuse we could think of on the spur of the moment,' she muttered. 'It made me uneasy from the start, and I hated it when it all kind of . . . mushroomed.'

'You lied and I *knew* you lied,' said Jassim ruefully. 'That's been the trouble all along. That's what's made me so antagonistic. I couldn't decide where the lies ended and the truth began.' He swished a foot around in the water. 'When the room boy told me you'd slept in the bedroom while

Howard had used the settee in the living-room, it confirmed what I'd suspected. Believe me, I wasn't quizzing the boy,' he said, when her head jerked up and she gazed at him with startled eyes. 'It didn't seem quite proper to waltz into the bunglaow on my own and start helping myself to your possessions, so I took him along, too. It was while I was collecting your clothes that he volunteered the information. Maybe he shouldn't have done, but in any hotel the activities, or non-activities, of the guests are common knowledge among the staff. You must have realised that after your first night the word would be spread about two beds having been slept in?' he said, when she continued to look nonplussed.

'I—we did, but there wasn't anything we could do about it.' He was not a snooper, Clemence thought gratefully. He had not picked up her passport. But if the knowledge he *had* picked up was not dealt with properly it could lead him down a very winding path. 'We felt it was our business. No one else's,' she explained. 'However——'

'It is,' Jassim cut in, and launched himself off the side the pool and back into the water.

With a splash, the conversation had been terminated. The opportunity to explain about her and Howard had gone. Jassim swam length after length after length, only stopping when Clemence attracted his attention to tell him Sunthi had called. Dinner was ready. Throughout the meal, and the rest of the evening, Clemence looked for a way to raise the subject again, but her host seemed intent on discussing everything else under the sun—books, films, his travels in Oman, her journeys throughout Europe. She was sidetracked and, it had to be admitted, most enjoyably.

The next morning she awoke with her aches and pains gone, and her mind made up. She would not be sidetracked again. Even if she and Jassim had set off on the wrong foot, all that was in the past. She would tell him she was single because . . . she *needed* him to know. And if Jassim then decided to move in closer she would have no objections. Not one.

But when she went through to breakfast she discovered that for the next couple of hours at least, her host was out of reach. A note had been left, full of apologies, but explaining that a crisis at the depot required his attention. He had to go. Sorry, there was no way out. And Jassim had no clear idea of when he would return.

Before showering Clemence had unwound what had diminished into a very grubby bandage and examined her fingers. They looked fine. A few chords plucked on an invisible harp proved they felt fine, too. The bandage was discarded. No longer hampered, she was able to help Sunthi with the breakfast dishes, much to his shy delight. After putting the crockery away as directed, she wandered off to spend time looking through a box of books Jassim had supplied. She was spoilt for choice. There were some of the modern novels they had touched upon the previous evening, *The Perfumed Garden*, three Arabian travel books and a copy of *The Rubaiyat of Omar Khayyam*. Where did she start?

Clemence was opening one of the travel books when an inscription on the flyleaf caught her eye. 'To my precious Jassim, with love, Roz', it read. Who was Roz? she wondered. The mysterious Mrs X or some girl he had left behind in Australia? A girl to whom he might intend to return. She frowned, awarding herself ten out of ten for stupidity. She had been so busy fitting Jassim into her life—being convinced that news of her availability would have had him drawing closer—that she had never stopped to

think how she might fit into his. He might not be interested
in drawing closer—not in any worthwhile way. Admittedly he appeared to be attracted, but if there had been few
females in his life recently chances were he would be
attracted to any girl who looked half-way decent. He was a
healthy male animal. Suppose what appealed was a
whirlwind romance which filled her time in Oman, but no
longer? She had had experience of such affairs before.

Jettisoning the book and muttering a disgruntled, 'No,
thanks,' she returned to the kitchen to find Sunthi
assembling ingredients for her lunch. A cold, clear soup was
on the menu, to be followed by flaky pastry shells in which
nestled prawns covered by a spicy sauce. Clemence loved to
cook, but a lifestyle which consisted of moving from one
location to another had allowed few opportunities. Now she
was eager to become involved, and her disgruntlement
faded as Sunthi, smiling broadly, allowed her to help. A
mixture of pidgin English, hand signals and much
laughter, produced lunch. Afterwards she helped with the
dishes again, and when there was still no sign of Jassim
settled down with the houseboy to make first preparations
for dinner's main dish—chicken with coriander.

The siesta came mid-afternoon. Not in the habit of
sleeping during the daytime Clemence decided chances of
her doing so now were small, and when she lay down with a
book it was in expectation of a good read. Not so. Within
minutes her eyes had closed, and when she next opened
them it was to find a sky tinged with delicate shades of rose-
petal, cream and lilac grey. She had been asleep almost
three hours.

In the kitchen, Sunthi was busy at the stove.

'Can I do anything to help?' she offered, miming her
appreciation of the chicken and coriander which was

already simmering, but he smiled and shooed her away.

'Boss,' he said, pointing to the back door.

'Swimming?' Clemence performed energetic movements.

He laughed and nodded.

Minutes later, she was marching barefoot across the warm stone of the courtyard in her bikini. Through the gate she went and into the garden. Yesterday they had swum earlier and sunshine had polished the greenery, glittered the water. Now dusk hung a diaphanous curtain. When she paused before the pool, the scene seemed almost mystical. In the deepest part, with his back towards her, she caught sight of Jassim. He was treading water. After a moment he ducked, then surfaced. His broad shoulders gleamed, his hair made a helmet of jet. Clemence's heart turned over.

He flung himself forward in a graceful crawl and, on reaching the far curve, raised himself on strong forearms. When he swung himself out of the water, her chest went tight, her pulse tripped. He was naked—very naked. Glorious with muscle, sinew and golden flesh, his body made a vibrant masculine statement. There was no comparison with the pale-skinned Ralph, nor lanky Howard. Jassim was an entirely different breed.

'Now we're quits,' he said, his voice making her jump. He lifted a towel and wrapped it around his hips. 'I usually head straight for the pool when I get back,' he explained, walking forward. 'And as Sunthi told me you were sleeping, I decided to follow my usual procedure.'

Clemence gave a tiny smile. 'Yes.'

'The crisis I mentioned in my note was a panic call from contractors laying foundations for a hospital. Never mind that it's Friday, the Moslem day of rest, they'd decided they were at a crucial stage and required urgent supplies of ready-mixed concrete. Six of our mixers started a ferrying service, then one broke down. So instead of enjoying the only twenty-four hours in the whole week which I can call my own, I find myself out in the desert fixing the damned engine.'

'You're a mechanic?' she enquired feebly.

'Among other things. Two hours wielding spanners and cleaning points in the blazing sun with the temperature soaring well over the hundred is no joke. By the time the engine was in operation again, the air was blue. Then another vehicle went down with a puncture. I needed to travel miles to collect a spare, and when I'd sorted that— guess what? One of the drivers isn't feeling too well. Can I take over? I ought to have known disasters come in threes.' Jassim frowned at her. 'Well, say something.'

What? How? Clemence's mouth was dry, her breath trapped in her lungs. She searched for a comment, an interested question, but nothing came. All she could do was gaze at the man before her; a muscular man with caramel-coloured skin and green eyes.

'Stop it! Stop it, Clem,' he ordered. 'Stop looking at me like that.'

'Like what?' she croaked.

Energy seemed to be flowing between them, an energy which drew, linked, compelled. Aware she must be staring at him as if he could turn straw into gold, she tried hard to summon up the willpower to look away, but was magnetised. Little by little they gravitated towards each other. Which of them made the final decisive move was uncertain, but suddenly she was in his arms. Fate seemed to have designed her body to slot into his, for Clemence could feel all of him—the muscled chest, flat stomach, the impact of his thighs. And when he kissed her, his mouth greedily tasting the honey of hers, liquid fire ran in her veins.

'Damn you,' Jassim muttered against her mouth, then stepped back. 'Damn you,' he said again, louder. He tugged at the towel knotted around his waist, and frowned. 'I notice you've thrown away the bandage, so presumably your wrist feels OK?' She gave a mute nod. 'Great, after dinner I'll drive you over to the hotel.'

'After dinner?' Clemence echoed blankly.

'You must want to get back to your harp.'

'Yes, I suppose so, but ——'

'And as you're being paid big money to provide music at the Plaza, the sooner you're providing it again, the better.'

She frowned, bewildered by this decision to ship her back post-haste. 'My wrist seems to be strong enough, but I don't know yet whether it'll stand up to a full session.'

'True, and the only way you'll find out is by practising. Which you can't do unless you and your harp are united.'

'Jassim, the doctor quoted a three or four-day recovery, so couldn't you take me back tomorrow?' She grinned appealingly. 'Me staying overnight isn't going to make much difference.'

'It could make all the difference,' he objected.

'How?'

He hesitated, then said at a rush, 'Howard's exact return date was never specified, right? So how's it going to look if he arrives tonight and you're not around?'

'Tonight?' Clemence gave a disbelieving laugh. 'No way. He isn't going to appear like a genie out of a bottle.'

'He might change his plans.'

'He won't, but even if he did turn up and discovered I was here with you, he wouldn't——'

Jassim wafted a hand. 'OK, OK, we've established you

and he are . . . free agents, but there's no point complicating matters. If you're there to greet him——'

'I'm expecting him next Wednesday, not before.' She frowned. Has he been trying to get in touch?'

'He hasn't. I rang through to the hotel switchboard this afternoon and asked. You've received no calls.'

'Then he definitely won't be returning to the Plaza this weekend.'

'But you will.'

'If I stayed a bit longer, even just overnight, it'd allow more credence to the story you give Mrs X,' she pointed out.

'That's not going to work. I've had a word. I said you were with me and——' Jassim looked beyond her shoulder, '—you turned me on, but all she did was call me a rascal. It was not,' he added drily, 'quite the reaction I was aiming for.'

'You did explain that Howard and I are——'

'Yes, though without reading her the small print. Look, if you were single she might well have regarded your appearance in my life as something serious. Because you're not, she doesn't. It's that simple.'

'No, it isn't,' Clemence protested. 'Agreed Howard and I go our separate ways, but that's because——'

'Another time.' He took a step towards the path. 'Dinner'll soon be ready, so if you want a swim you'd better jump in. I'll go and get dressed. Then as soon as we've eaten, we'll be off,' he declared, displaying brisk Australian gung-ho.

A stubborn little line appeared between her eyebrows. 'I'd be obliged if you would spare a moment to listen.'

Jassim shook his head. 'Like you said yesterday, it's your business. No one else's.'

As he turned and walked away, Clemence scowled.

What was going on? When he had suggested—no, insisted!—she take up residence in his house in the first place, her absence from the hotel and cancelled performances had not been an issue. Now he regarded every lost hour as vital. Why? Hearing how she and Howard shaped up together did not seem to be an issue, so could it be that in the midst of kissing her, he had recalled a lapsed allegiance to the girl who had written her name in his book—Roz?

Was guilt, and a belated wish to be loyal, at the back of this insistent need now to eject her?

'About me and Howard,' Clemence called, in one last desperate attempt.

'I'm not interested,' he flung back over his shoulder. 'All I *am* interested in is you having a swim, assembling your gear and eating dinner. In two hours' time I intend to have you back at the Plaza.'

'Don't I get any say in what *I'd* like to do?' she demanded.

Jassim stopped, swivelled and glared. 'On this occasion, Clemence, no, no, no!'

CHAPTER SEVEN

JASSIM had moved fast. After rushing through dinner, he had driven the jeep across the desert at breakneck speed, and at the hotel had almost pressed a hand against the small of Clemence's back in an attempt to propel her inside the bungalow. Dumping her suitcase at her feet, he had muttered a hurried goodbye. There was no strolling away this time. It had been more like a gallop. Hurt and indignant, Clemence had felt like burying her head in a pillow, or punching one. What she did do was return her clothes to the mirrored unit, wallow in a bath scented with the floral salts provided and later switch on the in-house video; but the comfort of her surroundings, so appealing from a distance, gave little joy.

Enquiries the next morning revealed that during her absence her harp had been kept in the store-room where she had previously practised, and after breakfast she went along to experiment with a few chords. As the chords sprouted into a tune and blossomed into a medley, it became clear the doctor's predicted recovery time had been overly pessimistic. Clemence's wrist and fingers were as flexible and capable as ever. All set to inform Khalid that she was ready, willing and able to play her music that evening, she was crossing the lobby in search of him when one of the desk clerks called. The man held out a telephone. Howard was on the line.

'I'm in a pay-phone and don't have much money, so this'll have to be brief,' he said, when she took the receiver. 'Apologies for not being in touch sooner, but I'm ringing to let you know you can expect me in Oman next weekend.'

'Next weekend? But I reckoned on Wednesday!' she hissed, wishing she could have taken the call somewhere less public than the reception desk. 'Huh, when you mentioned, a full month I should've known you'd take it. Next weekend, you say now, but will you stick to that or are you intending to leave me here to soldier on alone until our contract ends?'

'Clem, you have my solemn oath I'll be with you at the Plaza next weekend, even if I have to be dropped in by parachute.'

'Saturday or Sunday?' she demanded.

There was a pause as the pips sounded and Howard pushed more coins into the slot.

'Sunday. I'm trying for an early-morning flight, but the travel agents have yet to confirm. As soon as there's a fixed booking I'll be in touch. How are you? Been around and about with Otto yet? You've no idea how lucky you are to have sunshine. Here it's done nothing but rain—I got soaked yesterday! And it's cold. On television they've been saying how temperatures have hit an all-time low for this time of year.'

'Howard, the weather is the last thing which interests me.'

Beep, beep, beep, the pips went again.

'Sorry, no more money,' he told her merrily. 'Don't worry, I'll——'

The connection broke, the call ended. Clemence thrust down the receiver. Howard was unreliable, treacherous, a complete dead loss. Yvonne was welcome to him! She located a smile from somewhere to thank the clerk for his trouble and, now armed with *two* reasons for speaking to him, resumed her quest for Khalid. In view of what had happened at the beach, it seemed unlikely the young man would protest when she applied for an extension of her partner's leave of absence, she thought wryly. In all probability, remorse would have him offering red-faced regrets and agreeing to anything.

But Khalid, regretful or otherwise, was nowhere to be found in the lobby, nor could she spot him passing the time of day with anyone at the poolside. Deciding he must be in his second-floor office, Clemence took the elevator. She had emerged into the cloistered quiet of the management suite and was walking along a corridor, when Otto came out of a room ahead of her.

'The desert safari's already over?' he queried, his surprise at finding Clemence so quickly back at the hotel as great as hers had been.

She nodded and glanced along to a door marked 'K. Al Fori, Hotel Manager' in gold letters. 'I'm here to give notice that I'd like to resume my performances.'

'In that case I'll make sure Mr Varoop and his group are advised that they're no longer required. Overseeing the Plaza's entertainment programme is one of my duties now,' the Swiss explained, when Clemence looked puzzled. 'And, confidentially, it'll be a relief to have you on stage again. A taste for the Indian hit-parade is something I have yet to acquire!'

'I'm afraid it'll only be me on stage,' she apologised. 'Howard's just telephoned to say he's been delayed until next weekend.'

'Don't worry about it.'

'Thanks. Throughout his absence we've been credited with the full amount written into our contract,' said Clemence, eager to sort out finances and never mind if Howard preferred to accept all they could, 'but that's not giving the hotel a fair deal. I'd appreciate it if our earnings could be scaled down to take account of the situation.'

'Leave it. We'll discuss the matter when Howard returns.' He walked with her towards the elevator. 'And what are you serenading our guests with tonight?'

'I thought—Beatle music?'

Otto smiled. 'Can't be bad.'

It wasn't. Although Clemence began the evening wondering whether a full session on her harp might bring some undetected weakness in her fingers to light, her anxiety proved unfounded. All went well. At the close of her programme she was plucking the strings with as much strength and verve as at the start. This resumption of normality imparted a feeling of satisfaction—which was more than could be said for every other facet of her life.

Howard and his continuing disappearing trick rubbed like sandpaper, but the man who really ground her down was Jassim. His abrupt banishment of her remained an irritation, and a mystery. She could only assume he had been beset with memories of a girl back home. He had, she recalled, made a reference to telephone calls and visits to Brisbane. Did the girl live in Brisbane? But if there was a girl, did she matter that much? Clemence's feelings seesawed. She did not know how it had happened, but Jassim had become important to her and, deep down, she felt she was important to him. Never mind any other woman, he had kissed her as though he meant it. As though he cared. And if she had looked at him longingly, greedily, hadn't he done the same? He might have said goodbye, but he could not have *meant* goodbye, she assured herself. The two of them shared something, and that something would bring him back.

On stage on Saturday, her gaze swung around the lobby so many times that vertigo was in danger of setting in.

When he did not appear, she waited for Sunday. She waited in vain. Her assurance dented, Clemence pinned all her hopes on Monday, but the place where he had stood remained stubbornly vacant. The dents eroded into cavities. She sat out Tuesday. No Jassim. After suffering through Wednesday, she gave herself a stern little talk. For five days—ten performances—she had been keyed up and apprehensive, but it had to stop. The time had come to admit that she had been wrong, and that, whatever his reasons, when Jassim had said goodbye he had meant farewell, it's over, the end.

Clemence brushed rapidly through her hair and reached for her stetson. Even if it was the end, didn't common courtesy insist he should call to enquire if her wrist was OK, ask how she was feeling? One glare in the mirror to check that her cowgirl outfit was in order, then she marched out of the bungalow, heading for the lobby and her Thursday evening show. The Al Foris were short on common courtesy, she thought scathingly. It was a family failing. Jassim might have apologised for his past behaviour, but Khalid, the true villain of the piece, had yet to make amends. Indeed, in all the time she had been back at the Plaza she had not seen him once. The days of waylaying her, of wanting to chat, were long gone. The youth must now be on continual alert, sneaking behind pillars and darting into doorways whenever she walked through the hotel. She knew an apology represented a loss of face, but not to write a note or offer a single word of regret just wasn't good enough!

Catching sight of Otto on her way towards the stage, Clemence altered course.

'Could you tell where I can find Khalid?' she demanded. 'I'd like to have a word with him.'

'He isn't here.'

'Then I'd like to speak to him the moment he returns.'
Her wide-legged stance indicated determination. 'And if an
appointment is what it takes, I'll make one!'

'You can't. I mean, there's no point. Didn't you know?
Khalid's in America.'

Her blue-grey eyes opened wide. 'America?'

'San Francisco, to be precise.' The Swiss gave a wooden
bow. 'If you'd care to tell me the problem, I'll do my best to
handle it for you.'

'No—no, thanks. When did he go?'

'Last Friday afternoon. I understand he's enrolled for a
two-year course in hotel management and catering at a
college there, and not before time. Of course, he'll be
arriving mid-semester, but——' Otto lowered his voice and
glanced around to check he could not be overheard,
'between you and me, I suspect the arrangement was
impromptu. Certainly I'd never heard so much as a
whisper. Friday started with a stream of telephone calls
from the penthouse. Next thing, a limousine's ordered and
later a porter was instructed to collect half a dozen
suitcases. I presumed that despite her just returning, Mrs Al
Fori must be off on her travels again—each year she goes
the rounds of the European fashion houses—but instead
Khalid was driven to the airport. He looked very subdued.
When the bellboy asked if anything was wrong, he told him
he was in the cathouse. The cathouse!' There was an abrupt
guffaw. 'Whatever he's done, it must be something severe—
his mother would never send him away unless——' All of a
sudden, Otto glanced at the clock on the wall. 'I'm delaying
you.'

With a nod, Clemence concurred. She walked on stage,
took up her position at her harp, and started plucking the
strings. Outwardly her demeanour was calm, inside she
seethed. Cross-reference Khalid's departure with her being

pitchforked back to the hotel, and everything fell oh-so-neatly into place. She had been duped. The only reason Jassim had taken her to his house had been to keep her out of the way until his kid brother had had time to skip the country. His tale of requiring her presence to prise away Mrs X had been a sham. Mrs X—the evasive title ought to have aroused her suspicions. And the way he had later dismissed the scheme, saying it was not going to work, should have alerted her as well. Instead, Dumbo had been immune to the aroma of rat—a rat who, once Khalid's exit had been achieved, could not get rid of her fast enough. The boy could barely have been airborne before he had shuffled her back!

Fingers making sweet music, Clemence placed her performance on auto-pilot as she brooded over the events of the past week. So much for believing she was important to Jassim. She had been—so long as he could use her. After that—chop! But the chopping had not been restricted to her. Khalid had been severed from his homeland with indecent haste. Clearly Leyla Al Fori played a part, but what was the betting her stepson had been the prime mover? Yet why had he moved so fast? Otto had presumed Khalid had done something 'severe', but seen from the distance of a week the youth's attempted seduction fell far short of that category. Banishing him was too extreme. Everyone's allowed one error of judgement, Clemence thought, then stumbled over a note. Suppose Khalid was guilty of not *one* error, but several? Suppose he was in the habit of stealing women away? Suppose. Suppose. Suppose.

Engrossed in her thoughts, Clemence was acknowledging the applause at the end of her recital, when her eyes abruptly focused. A tall figure in khaki shirt and trousers was standing, one broad shoulder resting against the wall, watching her. After playing absentee for five nights in a

row, Jassim—the rat—had chosen to appear. In too much
of a hurry to tuck her sheet music inside its folder, she
grabbed everything up in a bundle and charged down from
the stage. The heels of her leather boots thudding, she made
a beeline across the white marble floor.

'What sublime timing!' she exclaimed, as she landed in
front of him. 'You're exactly the person I want to see.'

'I am?'

Just two words, but Clemence managed to wring
caution, watchfulness and doubt out of them. There was
also a moment when she wondered about an air of hope, but
as that did not fit she tossed it away.

'Yes. I hear you've exiled Khalid to America. Could you
explain why?'

Jassim pushed back the slouch hat. 'First of all, he isn't
exiled.'

'OK, you sent him,' she corrected, snappy with
impatience.

'Not me. The idea originated with Leyla, which is not to
say it doesn't meet with my full approval. It does. Though
my reasons for wishing him bon voyage are different from
hers. Khalid's gone over there to study hotel management.'

'You didn't listen to the question. I want to know *why* did
he go, not what for. It's because of the beach incident, isn't
it?' demanded Clemence, her voice rising.

Jassim frowned. 'Yeah. Leyla felt that in view of what
had happened with you——'

'Me, just me? Aren't you forgetting about Ingrid? And
who else? How many other unsuspecting females has
Khalid . . . befriended? Half a dozen? Twenty? All those
east of Suez and west of the Maldives?'

Her cavalry-like charge across the lobby had drawn
attention, but this outburst had guests and staff alike
beginning to take a close interest.

'Let's talk in your bungalow,' Jassim suggested, and placed his hand on her arm. 'Come on.'

In a fury, she shook him off. 'I won't come on! I'm not going anywhere with you. Oh!' In avoiding him, her hold on the music had loosened and now sheets were floating to the ground like so many rectangular snowflakes. 'This is all your fault,' Clemence stormed, and dropped to her knees to begin grabbing them up willy-nilly.

'Allow me.' Bending alongside, Jassim commandeered the papers and began to sort them in an orderly fashion. 'Want these in that folder you're clutching?' he enquired, busily topping and tailing.

'No.' He was too cool, too calm, too *organised*. She could not be bothered with the correct procedure for stacking the sheets away. 'What I want is a full explanation of——'

'Shh!' As before, the blocking index finger was raised.

'I won't shh!'

'Clem, you might not care that we're providing a floor-show, but I do,' he said, rising to his feet. 'So I'd prefer it if we continued this conversation outside where it's more private.' He handed her the music and strode off. At the glass doors, he glanced over his shoulder. 'That is, if you want to continue it,' he threw back, when he saw she was hesitating.

Clemence scuttled after him. What else could she do?

'The incident a week ago was the latest in a series, wasn't it?' she demanded, as they went on to the terrace. 'And the reason your baby brother's been shoved off to the States is that you and his mother are terrified this practice of his might prove fatal.' She thrust him a poison arrow of a look. 'You said the rules in Oman were harsh. What happens to addicted philanderers and rapists, are they stoned to death?'

Jassim sighed. 'Khalid's neither of those, and you know it.'

'Do I? OK, I agree I came to no harm, but what about the others?'

'There haven't been any others.'

'No? What about poor Ingrid?'

'Poor Ingrid?' His voice curdled. 'If there was an Olympic medal for calculating bitches, that woman would take gold every time!'

'And in my opinion Khalid would race home in the men's event! I reckon——'

Clemence was all set to carry on her attack when her companion shot a look down to the pool-area and scowled. It was a silencing scowl. Two businessmen were approaching, taking a route which skirted them. Frustrating as it was, she forced herself to keep quiet until they disappeared. All ready to start up again, she had done no more than take a deep breath when Jassim intervened.

'I refuse to stand here and chew the fat while the rest of mankind listens on, so as you've made it clear you're not prepared to come anywhere with me,' he said drily, 'suppose you lead while I follow? And wherever you settle for, I'd be grateful if you could see your way clear to making a detour past your bungalow and ditching that music. The way you're holding it, one breath of wind'll scatter it to the four corners of the earth.'

Clemence clasped what seemed to have grown into sufficient sheets to score an entire symphony tighter to her chest, and stomped off down the steps.

'Ingrid's a bitch and Khalid's Little Boy Blue, is that what you're telling me?' she derided, as they walked through the gardens.

'No. Khalid takes his share of the blame. Though I should point out that whereas for him it was lust at first sight, for her the buzz-word was greed. Khalid and his wealth were to Ingrid what raw flesh is to the mako shark. And as she didn't have two scruples to rub together, any qualms about obtaining money in a horizontal rather than an upright way were eliminated.'

'Where did he meet her?'

'Here, at the Plaza.'

'Let me guess, she played the harp?'

'She just wandered in each evening and spent time in the bar,' he said, his glower showing the barb had been effective. 'However, she was a blonde and pretty. I guess that's something else that threw me with you. I saw similarities. OK, so I needed glasses,' added Jassim, with a spark of belligerence.

'A white stick.'

They had reached Clemence's bungalow, and here they stopped in the pool of golden light thrown by an old-style gas-lamp.

'Khalid had been burned once,' he explained. 'I sure as hell wasn't going to allow the boy to get burned again.'

'As you thought!'

'As I thought. Look, with you and Howard telling tales, I felt compelled to check you out. Wouldn't you have done the same?'

Clemence sighed. 'Well ... yes,' she admitted.

'There was no way I could babysit you all the time, but I reckoned if you were on stage at six o'clock each evening nothing too dreadful could have happened.' Jassim stopped talking. With narrowed eyes, he looked beyond her shoulder, along the path and into the shadows. For a moment or two, he searched the darkness. 'Ingrid had flirted with Khalid, led him to believe she was infatuated,' he said, returning his attention. 'So he invited her down to the beach.'

'Khalid pretended there was a barbecue?'

'No, it was a straightforward invitation to join him in a twosome. She knew exactly what'd be involved. She knew——' again Jassim stopped mid-flow to peer into the darkness, '—he'd want to kiss her, like this.'

When he gathered her up in a bear-hug and his mouth came down on hers, Clemence was stunned. She could not believe it. One second he had been talking in a sombre and matter-of-fact fashion, the next he was holding her tight, kissing her as though his life depended on it. There was no thought for the crumpling and creasing of the sheet music which was trapped between them, no thought for the crumpling and creasing of her emotions. Head spinning, she attempted an escape, but his grip would not slacken. The kiss went on and on and on, and somewhere along the way his lips parted hers. What had been a one-sided event turned into combined effort.

At last Jassim came up for air. 'Thanks,' he said. He took one hasty glance along the curve of the path, and frowned. The next thing Clemence knew, she was being trundled backwards up to the bungalow until he had her pressed against the door.

'Where's the key?' he muttered, and kissed her again.

'I don't think——'

'The key,' he insisted. Her stetson was threatening to fall off, so he raised a hand and tilted it back on to her head. 'Where's the bloody key?'

'Jassim, we——'

Under cover of a third kiss, he slid his fingers to probe into first one of her waistcoat pockets, then the other. Having located the key, he moved swiftly. Before she could protest, he had bundled her inside the bungalow and closed the door behind them.

'Thanks,' he said again. The room was dim, lit by a

golden beam from outside, but his smile shone through the darkness. 'Thanks for co-operating.'

'Co-operating in—in what?' Clemence felt weak and drained and lightheaded.

'Deceiving Mrs X.'

She groaned. 'You don't still expect me to believe that stupid woman exists, do you?'

'But she *does*. Clem, she was out there. My guess is she noticed us talking in the lobby and followed. If previously she didn't believe we were—serious, seeing us in each other's arms is bound to make her think again.'

Clemence thrust the motley heap of music and folder on to the desk and turned. The moment had been utilised to recoup her strength, and now she glared.

'I must have been crazy to trust you before, but don't think I'll fall for the same trick twice. You kept me at your house under false pretences. It had nothing to do with the so-called Mrs X, and everything to do with Khalid.'

'Incorrect.' He strode to the window and drew the curtains, then switched on the light. 'Did I *keep* you there?' he asked, as he returned to her side. 'No way. Think back. After you went walkabout wasn't it me who was eager to return you to the hotel, and wasn't it you who said no?'

'You engineered it so I had the impression I was making the decision myself, but that's what all good con artists do.'

'Bull! How could I get a girl like you to——'

Clemence talked over him. 'You pretended to give me a choice then, but it's noticeable how I wasn't allowed to voice an opinion when you wanted me to leave later. Of course! I remember now how you said you phoned the Plaza on Friday afternoon. You reckoned you were enquiring whether Howard had been trying to get in touch, but——'

'I was.'

'Huh!' she retorted, and Jassim shrugged, prepared to ride this one out. 'My bet is you called to check whether Khalid had been removed from harm's way. He had, so then it was a case of eat your dinner, Clem, get in the jeep, and beat it,' she said, not bothering to keep the hurt from her voice.

He removed his slouch hat. 'If you'd stayed it would have been——' he frowned, turning the hat in his hands, '—disastrous or wonderful, whichever way you care to look at it. I'll explain later,' he mumbled, and flicked the hat on to the desk with her music. 'First I want to clear up this business of Ingrid. She went to the beach with Khalid where there were high jinks, and subsequently the pair of them travelled on to a house my stepmother owns in the south. But at no stage did the question of kidnap arise. I understand the woman did start by acting coy, but that was tactics, because later it was she who suggested that a few days alone together would be fun. Khalid remembered about Leyla's house standing empty, and off they went.' He was speaking matter-of-factly again, using a tone which left Clemence no alternative but to calm down. 'The first I heard was when Leyla phoned me at work the next morning, frantic because Khalid had disappeared. She has a fetish about keeping track of him and when, as usual, she'd demanded to know his plans the previous night he had said he was going to the bay, though he'd reckoned it was with a mate—a male one. However, someone had noticed him leaving the hotel with Ingrid. Leyla has connections throughout Oman and by making discreet enquiries we managed to establish that Khalid's car had been seen travelling south. As the house seemed an obvious location, I drove down there. When I confronted them Ingrid was taken by surprise and admitted that the excursion had been her idea. After a night to think things over her story changed.' Jassim riffled his fingers through his hair. 'Not only did she portray Khalid as an under-age sex maniac with psychopathic tendencies and threaten to call in the police——'

'As I did.'

'I guess,' he acknowledged curtly, '—she also vowed she'd sell her story to the highest bidder. Can't you imagine the fun the Western tabloids would have had with, "Innocent Blonde Seized By Rapacious Arab Juvenile"?' He spoke in cryptic headlines. 'This had Leyla indulging in a grand display of histrionics, that's her style, but the moment she calmed down she negotiated a financial settlement.'

Clemence picked up his disdain. 'You didn't agree?'

'No. There wasn't one scrap of evidence to substantiate what Ingrid had said. And, God Almighty! a sniffer dog with a bad cold could have detected her motives in two seconds flat. I made strong protests, but Leyla was adamant it was her show.' He grimaced. 'By dishing out cash she smoothed the matter over, but seems to have left Khalid with the impression he could be bailed out another time, if necessary.'

'Wasn't he warned—surely he must have known—he'd be in big trouble if anything similar happened again?'

'He was. He did. I pointed out the realities in no mean way and his mother assured me she had, too. Yet I can only assume she soft-pedalled because—what d'ya know?—the bloody kid goes and makes advances to you. Leyla's great on screaming and shouting, but rarely follows through. You do believe all of this?' Jassim demanded abruptly.

'Yes,' said Clemence, startled. She did believe him— where Khalid and Ingrid were concerned. Mrs X remained a more dubious matter.

'Good. I'd hate to think I've been wasting my breath. Mind if I sit down?'

'Go ahead.'

When he dropped himself down on the rattan sofa, Clemence decided she might as well be comfortable, too. Removing her stetson, she perched herself on the other end.

'I wasn't intending to tell you this, it seemed like an added nail in the kid's coffin, but now he's gone and——' Jassim shrugged, '—and I'd like to clear up the matter once and for all.' He leant forward, his hands clasped between his knees. 'Remember I asked if you'd ever come across Khalid before? Well, you may not have seen him, but it turned out he'd seen you.'

'He had? Where?'

'In London last year. I'd mixed up the timing. It was late February he'd been there, not March.'

Clemence pursed her lips. 'February must have been when Howard and I were appearing in the rooftop restaurant at the Galaxy.'

'That's right. Khalid and Leyla occupied one of their suites.' He shot her a rueful glance. 'The business about the Plaza booking Harrell & Co apparently at random and for an exorbitant fee had been troubling me, so while Leyla had Khalid on the rack I took the opportunity to turn a screw or two myself. It appears the boy had seen you playing your harp and liked what he saw. His version is that, because your relationship with Howard had seemed——' Jassim moved his shoulders, '—flimsy, he felt you could be amenable to an approach. Obviously there was no opportunity to approach you in London, not with his mother riding shotgun, so he asked around, discovered the name of your agent, and you know the rest.'

'What made Khalid decide Howard and I were— flimsy?' she enquired.

He opened his hands to stretch long tanned fingers, then clasped them tight again. 'It seems there was another guy hanging around. The two of you were often together, but Howard didn't mind.'

'I don't remember anyone,' Clemence muttered, trying to recall the time at the Galaxy.

'He was quite a bit younger than you. Oh, and he had a motorbike, an old black one. Khalid followed you down to the car park one evening after your show and saw you go off on it together.'

She laughed. 'Mystery solved!'

Jassim looked unimpressed. 'Khalid regarded your admirer's youth as a bonus. It gave him the idea you preferred younger men.'

'Boys just out of school?' Clemence grimaced. 'Like to know who it was I rode off with?'

'Not particularly.'

'His name was Pete. He's my teenage brother.'

'Your brother?' In an instant change of mood, Jassim sat up and grinned.

'The one and only. Pete's tall and skinny, and has spiky hair. He lives in patched jeans and tee-shirts with spider's webs and skeletons on them.' She wobbled her head in despair. 'And Khalid decided he was my lover!'

'Khalid tends to be naïve,' he said, his green eyes gleaming.

'Not that naïve.' In the midst of comic-tragic groans, Clemence sobered. 'Picking me out at the Galaxy, and subsequently bringing me all the way to Oman with the intention of pursuit, is only a whisker away from downright wicked.'

'It was unforgivable, which is why I maintain that what happened with you was his fault, and his alone. Unfortunately the boy considers he's a law unto himself at times. That's the way Leyla's brought him up. Because he's her very own Boy Wonder, she seems to have instilled the idea

that if he wants something he's entitled to it. She operates
on that basis herself,' added Jassim, with a bark of mirthless
laughter. 'Eighteen months ago being in charge of the
Plaza took Khalid's fancy, so disregarding his youth and
complete lack of training, his mother agreed.'

'It must be heady stuff, owning a place like this at his
age,' Clemence commented, and thought, not for the first
time, how unfair it seemed for Jassim to have so little when
his young brother had so much.

'True.' He shrugged. 'Still, two years in the States should
teach him the sun doesn't rise and set for Khalid Al Fori.
And breaking the ties with his mother could be the best
thing which ever happened to him. That's why I endorsed
the decision he should go.' Jassim grinned crookedly.
'Leyla's sent him over there to keep him out of trouble, but
my guess is he'll get into trouble and be well and truly
slapped down.' His grin widened. 'Or should it be kneed
down? The impact you had on his nether regions made him
stop and think. Add a couple of similar experiences and
he'll soon get the message.'

'Sounds a painful way to take instruction.'

Jassim laughed. 'Rather him than me!'

'And you've never heard anything more from Ingrid?'
she asked, after a pause.

'Not a word. Once the woman had received her haul, she
took off like a bullet-train. My guess is she's living it up
somewhere with her latest lover.'

'She was single?' Clemence asked, He nodded. 'Then on
what basis did she enter Oman?'

'Her brother worked in oil here, and she came as his
guest. Mind you, as he operated out in the sticks and she
preferred the bright lights, they rarely met. But the guy
had served his purpose. She couldn't have gained entry
without him.'

'Like I couldn't have gained entry without Howard.'

'Mmm,' he agreed vaguely. 'Though Howard's not your brother.'

'No.' It seemed to have gone very quiet all of a sudden. 'He's not my brother, but—but he's not my husband, either.'

His head jerked round. 'What?'

'We aren't married. We never have been. We're not Mr and Mrs Harrell at all.'

Jassim stared. 'You mean——'

'I'm single, and in Oman under false pretences. Howard did write me down as his wife, but only because Bernie, our agent, reckoned it was a widespread practice used to ease admission.' She sighed. 'Regardless of any chance of working here on some kind of legitimate single person's permit, I've fraudulently arrived as a married woman— which makes me an illegal immigrant.'

'A wetback? Who the hell cares? You're unattached? There's no reason why I shouldn't—why we shouldn't——' He burst out laughing. 'Oh, Clem, why didn't you tell me this?'

'How could I? At the start you were so hostile I was afraid that——'

'Forget it,' he said impatiently. 'It doesn't matter. What matters is that I'm not hostile now, and you're not married, and——' He grabbed her from the corner of the settee, and put his arms around her. 'Whatever there was between you and Howard is over, isn't it?'

Being held close made keeping track of the conversation difficult. Instead of confining herself to rational thought, Clemence became engrossed in marvelling at the cheek which was so near to hers. Smooth and smelling faintly of lemon, it contained that intriguing dimple.

'Er—yes——' she managed to reply. 'It's already been

decided that when we finish this stint in Oman, Harrell &
Co dies the death. The partnership's being dissolved.'

'So you won't be seeing him again?' Jassim demanded.

'Oh, I'll have to see him. I mean, I want to see him, but
only because——'

'Because there'll be the odd loose end to be dealt with on
the business side? Fine, I can live with that,' he said, and
once again he kissed her.

This time, the kiss felt different. Almost bruising with
certainty, it was a declaration of Jassim laying claim to *his*
woman. A hand on either side of her face, his fingers
entwined in the blonde mist of her hair, he held her captive,
a prisoner to the probing delights of his tongue. By the time
he raised his head, Clemence was breathless.

'Hey, wait a minute!' she gasped.

'Why wait? We've wasted far too much time already. Do
you know, thoughts of you have kept me awake every night
for weeks? I've been unable to get you out of my mind.'

'You wanted to get me out of your house, and with
unflattering speed,' she reminded him, pressing her hands
against his chest in order to forestall another onslaught.
'Why? Surely you could have taken my word when I said I
wasn't going to report Khalid? Surely you knew I wasn't
dangerous?'

'Sunshine, you were. Not in relation to Khalid, in
relation to me.' Jassim relaxed his hold, and put an arm
around her shoulder. 'From the start you attracted me like
hell.'

Clemence gave him an old-fashioned look. 'You had a
funny way of showing it!'

'Why else do you think I kissed you in the gardens? It was
the first time in my life I'd ever pounced on a strange
woman. I didn't want to, random carnality's not my style,
but I *had* to.' He shook his head in wonderment. 'Being out

of control like that made me bloody angry.'

'But you were so cool you almost walked away whistling!'

'Cool? The build-up of heat had me damn near exploding there and then! If I did make a nonchalant exit, it was only because my legs were in danger of buckling.' He bent to rub his brow against hers. 'That's one instance of when desire got the better of me, but there's a whole catalogue.'

'Like?' she demanded, breathless with the thrill of knowing she had this effect on him.

'Like when you flung your arms around me at the beach, like later that night when we stopped for water, like you appearing at the pool in that tiny white bikini when I was naked.' Jassim gave a tortured groan. 'Clem, when a man's aroused he stops thinking with his brain. At least, this one does. It's another part of his anatomy which guides him.'

She laughed. 'Is it?'

'Yes! And don't you dare act dumb and ask which,' he warned. 'I knew that if you spent the night under my roof, I'd be compelled to come to your bed. But how could I, when as far as I was concerned you were married? I'd realised Howard had left you in the lurch,' he continued, when she started to protest, 'but making love to a married woman went against the grain. I refuse to become involved in situations where I won't be morally comfortable, which meant I had to turf you out.' His fingertips moved to the deep vee neck of her waistcoat to gently caress the high curve of her breasts. 'That's what's kept me away all this week.'

'So why have you come back now?'

The fingers smoothing her breasts were making it difficult to sit still. Clemence ached. She blossomed. She felt all woman. And as he undid one button, and then two, she sighed.

'Because I can't help myself.'

When Jassim slid her waistcoat from her shoulders, she was naked beneath.

'God, you're beautiful,' he muttered, and as his mouth returned to hers, his hands moved to cup her breasts.

Held close, Clemence entwined her arms around his neck and began returning his kisses, fervour for heated fervour. She slid her fingers beneath his shirt and spread them, eager for the feel of his smooth firm flesh. She had never known such a yearning to touch. She wanted to touch all of him— naked. Should she? Dare she? She began by unbuttoning his shirt, but in seconds Jassim lost patience and tore the garment away. And then her hands were free to move in an ecstasy of delight across his wide shoulders, across his muscled chest.

'You're beautiful, too,' she whispered.

She felt, rather than saw, his smile.

'Never so appealing as you.'

Wanting more than to fondle the silken underswell of her breasts, his hands slid up to capture her nipples between his fingertips. The touch had Clemence murmuring in incoherent delight, and when he increased the sensual pressure, her head fell back and she moaned. Raw desire licked along her limbs, swelled her breasts with their taut tips, intensified the ache, that wonderful ache. She moved beneath him. In response Jassim bent his head, and the tongue which had sensually stroked her mouth now lapped at her nipples, making them even tauter, tighter, more sensitive than ever. Arched into his body, she was dizzy with need.

'Jass. Oh, Jass!'

'Clem. My darling, I——' The shrill of the telephone

froze the endearment, and changed it into an oath. 'Leave it,' he begged, feeling her hesitation. 'Let it ring.'

She waited, but when the sound came again and again she shook her head. 'I can't.'

With a sigh, Jassim pushed himself upright. 'Come back soon,' he implored as she crossed to the desk.

'I will.' Some quirk of modesty had her reaching for her waistcoat, and she was pulling it on as she picked up the phone. 'Hello?' she said weakly.

'Hi, Clem. It's the long-lost guitar-player.'

Jassim was waiting with elbows on his knees, his dark head sunk into his hands, and when she said, 'It's Howard!' he looked up and frowned.

'I'll be with you tomorrow.' her partner continued.

'Tomorrow?' She gave a laugh of surprise. 'Not Sunday?'

'You prefer Sunday?'

'No, no, come tomorrow. Please make it tomorrow.'

'I will. I've loused you up far too long already, but it was for a reason, Clem—an excellent reason. You see, two days ago Yvonne and I were married.'

'Married!' she exclaimed.

'You knew we were planning to get round to a ceremony some time,' he rebuked. 'And with the baby due in six months, it was obvious I'd prefer to make an honest woman out of the little love sooner rather than later. The day after I arrived, Yvonne confessed how much she hated the idea of us waiting until you and I came back from Oman. She pointed out that now was the ideal opportunity to apply for a special licence and get hitched. Yes?' he insisted.

'Yes,' said Clemence, wryly thinking how her suspicions of an ulterior motive had been on target.

'Wish us luck?'

'I do,' she said, and smiled. The brunette might be the last

woman in the world she would have chosen for Howard,
yet there seemed little doubt she would make him happy.

'You're pleased?'

'I'm pleased. I'm delighted. It's fantastic,' Clemence
vowed. She was stretching things a bit, but it would have
been niggardly not to give the new bridegroom what he
wanted. 'You're a great guy, and——' saying that Yvonne
was a great gal stuck in her throat '—and I know from
now on everything will be wonderful.'

'It will,' Howard agreed contentedly. 'And for you as
well.'

'How for me?'

'One of these days it'll be your turn to meet someone
special,' he prophesied. 'Someone who make you feel warm
inside. Someone you'll want to be with all day and every
day. Someone you're driven mad to touch, to hold, to——'

'I must go,' a low voice intruded, and she saw that Jassim
had risen. He was tucking the shirt so rapidly dispensed
with just as rapidly back into his trousers.

As Howard continued with an impassioned description
of her future beloved who was really his present beloved,
she placed her hand over the mouthpiece.

'Why?' Clemence implored.

'They'll be expecting you in the bar for your second
show.'

'That's not for another——'

'Clem, are you still there?' demanded Howard.

'Yes,' she said, watching in dismay as Jassim strode to the
door.

'Say after me, "I am going to feel warm inside",'
instructed the new bridegroom.

She sighed. Whether marriage was responsible or a
surfeit of celebration, he had become uncharacteristically
skittish all of a sudden.

'I don't——' she began.

'Say it.'

'I am going to feel warm inside,' she rattled off, as Jassim opened the door. 'Wait,' she begged.

'Sunshine, there's nothing to wait for.'

'There is!'

'No.'

'Yvonne's dreading my departure, even though I'll be back with her for good in four weeks,' Howard announced into a vacuum. 'I've told her the time'll soon pass, but she reckons it'll seem like a four-year prison sentence. Still, if I write every day and ring at least three times a week that should cheer her up.' Getting no response, he continued, 'I trust you intend to come to the airport and welcome back the prodigal? How about taking a note of the flight number and time?'

'Jass, you can't leave like this,' Clemence protested.

'Got a pencil handy?' enquired Howard.

'I don't see the point in——' The brim of the slouch hat was yanked down, shadowing his eyes. 'Sunshine, it's become patently clear we don't have a future.'

'No future? But why? What do you mean?'

'I'm due to arrive at twenty-three-fifty, that's ten minutes to midnight,' Howard said pedantically. 'If you order a taxi to take you out to the airport about half an hour after your second show, that'll allow ample time to——'

'Howard, shut up!'

It was too late. Jassim had gone.

'Why should I shut up?' a plaintive voice enquired. 'This isn't sour grapes, is it? I know you aren't ecstatic over Yvonne, but there's no need to get uptight. OK, you and I had a good thing going, but all good things come to an end.

Such is life. Clem, are you there?'

'I'm here,' Clemence said wearily, and reached for a ballpoint. 'Sorry I snapped. It had nothing to do with Yvonne. Now, tell me the details again.'

The details were provided, to be followed by a five-minute soliloquy on what a wonderful wife he had found himself. Costly telephone calls were permitted when extolling the brunette's virtues, it seemed. Released at last, Clemence slumped in the corner of the sofa. Why had Jassim changed from ardent lover to escapist in less than five minutes? she wondered dejectedly. What had prompted his determination to leave? Howard's phone-call must be involved somewhere. If only the blond guitarist hadn't rung *then*. If only he hadn't interrupted those wonderful moments when Jassim had been kissing her, and fondling her, and undressing her. If only he hadn't called when she had been totally engrossed in falling in love.

In love? The tempo of her heartbeat quickened. Her mouth went dry. She was in love with Jassim. She loved him. From the first she had been fascinated, intrigued, always aware when he had been around—she had never known a man with such power to arouse her every sense— and now Clemence acknowledged that those emotions had been the beginnings of love. Jassim Al Fori was her 'someone special'. He made her feel warm inside. She wanted to be with him all day and every day. Desire throbbed a silent beat. She wanted to touch him. To hold him. But he had walked out with no more than a vague reference to them having no future. Why?

Having picked up the gist of her conversation with Howard, had he been visualising *their* marriage and foreseen problems? What problems? There were no problems, she thought stubbornly. If he wanted to remain in Oman, that suited her. Though something would need to be done to upgrade his house. Alternatively, they could buy a place in Australia, or in England, or—— Realisation was swift and sharp. All of a sudden, Clemence understood. Upgrading a property cost money, likewise buying one. And as a mechanic-cum-relief driver, Jassim would not have the necessary cash.

She heaved a sigh. All men had a proud streak, and maybe Arabs more than most. Had he been making a dignified withdrawal because his Arab blood dictated that he could not, would not, invite her to share his life unless he was able to do so with style? But she didn't want style, all she wanted was Jassim.

She sat up straight. They needed to talk about this. She must make him understand money didn't matter. Clemence was in the middle of mentally persuading him the best things in life come free, when the telephone rang. Instantly she felt spine-tinglingly alive. In the time it took to lift the receiver, she had listened to Jassim's declarations of regret for his hasty departure, to declarations of how it would take far more than a zero bank balance to keep them apart, to declarations of his love.

'Hello?' she said tremulously.

'Good evening,' a tinkly female voice replied. 'My name if Leyla Al Fori. I feel it's time we met. Are you free tomorrow morning?'

'Um—yes,' said Clemence, nearly strangled by surprise.

'Then we shall take a drive. I'll be waiting at the front of the hotel at eleven o'clock sharp. Is that suitable?'

'Um—yes,' Clemence repeated.

The line went dead.

CHAPTER EIGHT

GLEAMING white, Muscat baked like a meringue in the sunshine. Hemmed into a natural bowl by stark mountains, the higgledy-piggledy squash of buildings within the city walls exuded a magic which had Clemence spellbound. The architecture, a fulsome blend of Arab, Persian and Indian, meant every house, every street, had a character of its own. Every garden was different, too. Not dusty wasteland here—there were wide lawns and shady dells, groves and gazebos. Bougainvillaea flowed in purple rivers over sugar-white walls, palm trees stood like green sentinels, even the traffic islands were bright with tropical flowers. With its fresh paint and attention to detail, Muscat proudly proclaimed itself as a Middle Eastern showplace. Everything was neat, everything shone—the glazed azure-blue domes of the mosques, the cannons lined up outside the Sultan's palace, the brass spear-points which topped the railings.

'They look as if they've been polished by hand,' Clemence remarked, snatching an admiring glance as they drove by.

'They have,' Leyla confirmed.

How Clemence wished her hostess would tap the uniformed chauffeur on his shoulder and stop the car. Her camera, regarded as an essential for the trip, had been held at the ready for ages, and given half a chance she would have had it swooping everywhere—from the fretted stone lace of the minarets, to the palace's elegant arcades, to the Portuguese fortress on the hill, a reminder of past foreign rule. But there had been no chance. When she had hinted that, being an unashamed tourist, she would like to take photographs, Leyla had muttered something about her not wearing a hat, and that was that. Mad dogs might brave the merciless sun, young women should know better than to ask. The refusal had surprised her, though the morning was rapidly turning out to be one surprise after another.

A 'dramatic-looking woman' had been Jassim's description of his stepmother, but in no way had he prepared her for the reed-slim fashion-plate whose manicured hand had so majestically summoned her to the luxurious depths of a silver Mercedes an hour earlier. Mathematics insisted that Leyla Al Fori must be nudging forty, if not beyond it, yet the oval face beneath the cloud of raven-black hair bore scant traces of the passing of time. How much credit could be attributed to the meticulously applied cosmetics, to the ministrations of masseurs and beauticians, was hard to say, but her brow was smooth and the skin which covered the blushered cheekbones taut. Her appearance was chic. No veils or cumbersome robes for her. Swathed in a pale green chifffon creation which advertised *haute couture* with every stitch, she was the epitome of the international socialite.

Having decided Leyla's invitation must be in lieu of the apology her son had never given, Clemence had climbed into the limousine expecting to be greeted with smiles, a wish to please, and—yes—a certain humility. She could not have been more wrong. Dark eyes had flashed, blatantly assessing her looks and her figure, and pricing her yellow tee-shirt and trousers; pricing them low. There had been a thin greeting, a precise command to the driver, and they were on their way. Her hostess's English, though accented, was fluent, yet Clemence's attempts at small talk had met road blocks in the form of a 'Yes' or a 'No' and silence. Indeed, the only time a comment had been volunteered was when Leyla had been fussing with her carefully coiffured hair.

'How do you manage such a glorious sheen?' she had enquired, in a manner which rebuffed an answer. 'If I ever come on earth again, I shall instruct Allah to make me a blonde.'

There seemed little doubt Allah would obey. The imperial gestures, the haughty disdain, warned Clemence that everything Jassim had said about his stepmother had been right. She was a force to be reckoned with. As the silence between them had solidified, so Clemence's bewilderment had grown. The woman was occupied with her own thoughts, and clearly not in the mood for either spouting regrets or acting the guide; so why had she organised this excursion?

A silversmith's shop caught Clemence's eye. There was a quick cameo of a robed man disappearing into an alley way. She saw a youngster mounting a donkey.

'Can't we stop?' she pleaded, in the hope of salvaging something from this non-event.

'We stop in a minute,' Leyla Al Fori decreed.

The Mercedes had been weaving along one narrow street after another, but suddenly they swung around a corner into a private and exclusive domain. Straight ahead, behind a knee-high stone wall and patch of lush lawn, Clemence saw a long, low, ranch-style house. Painted pristine white, and with contrasting black wrought-iron scrolls over the windows, the focal point was an arched porch where a vast array of pot plants flourished. The chauffeur drove on to the semi-circular drive and halted amidst the greenery.

A hand flicked in Clemence's direction. 'Come.'

Her hostess climbed from the car to accept the frilly parasol the driver proffered. Why a parasol should be required when they were already in the shade, Clemence did not know. What she did know was that in contrast to the cool green vision which was floating towards the

beautifully carved front door, she felt like a disgruntled
banana. A wrought-iron bell-pull was given a delicate tug,
generating a distant jangle. A lengthy silence followed,
during which the older woman took a powder-compact
from a green fabric purse. The peach bloom of her skin, the
shaped brows, the painted eyelids were examined in turn,
to her satisfaction, then she replaced the compact and
directed her gaze to Clemence. Once again the mascaraed
eyes were thorough, and unimpressed.

'Someone's at home,' Clemence heard herself say, when
at last sounds came from the interior. It was a stupid
observation, but the strain of being under scrutiny meant
she had had to say *something*. 'They're unbolting the door,'
she added inanely.

In what seemed to be slow and very noisy motion, the
door was unlocked. Forced to peer around the edge of the
parasol, for her hostess had positioned herself midway on
the marble step, Clemence watched it open. A tousled dark-
haired man, barefoot and dressed only in black pyjama
trousers, looked out.

'What the hell do you want, Leyla?' he enquired, batting
away a yawn. But when his sleepy green eyes collided with
those of blue-grey, the yawn became a strangled croak.
'Clem, what are you doing here?'

'*I* brought her,' his stepmother announced, spinning her
parasol in a way which, whether by accident or design, left
Clemence with no option other than to leap aside. 'You've
been drooling over this—harpist,' she spat out the word as
though Harrell & Co were a flaky vaudeville act, 'so I
decided the only way to make you understand that she isn't
what she seems was to bring her here, and——'

'It may have escaped your attention, but today happens
to be Friday, my one day of rest,' he interrupted. 'Last week
a firm of disorganised builders conspired to wreck my lie-
in, which meant I was looking forward to spending this

morning in bed—asleep.'

'It has gone noon.'

'I don't doubt it, but I happen to be tired.' Jassim rubbed his fists into his eyes. 'And in no mood for a confrontation or whatever it is you have in mind. I'd be grateful if the pair of you would kindly get back in the car, and go!'

Leyla never moved an inch. 'You need to know what this creature is.'

'I don't *need* to know anything,' came the growl.

'She's a reject, Jassim. A has-been. You said she and her husband were likely to part, but did you——'

'I remember what I said, but I got it wrong, and now you've got it wrong. Just forget the whole thing, Leyla.' He jerked a thumb at the Mercedes. 'Your chariot awaits, so leave!'

'Not until you've heard me out!'

'Excuse me. Am I to understand that the reason for this excursion is to—to . . . annihilate me?' asked Clemence, grappling for words in her amazement.

There was a heave of a bosom, a flaring of nostrils. 'I'm acting in Jassim's best interests. He must be made aware you're not at all the right girl for him.'

The sheer audacity of the reply had her choking with indignation. Why Leyla Al Fori should pry into her stepson's lovelife she had no idea, but clearly any woman who strayed into his sights was regarded as *her* business. And Clemence, having been vetted, was about to be vetoed!

'You see yourself as some kind of do-gooder?' she enquired, her voice as clipped and taut as a topiary hedge.

'In time he'll thank me for it,' replied Leyla, failing to pick up on the sarcasm.

'You have the most incredible gall!'

'And no sense of reality,' Jassim intruded. 'Thanks, Leyla, but no matter how much of a kick you derive from your cymbal-clashing dramas, this is neither the time nor the place.'

'I agree.' Three fingers lightly touched a brow which would never demean its owner by sweating. 'I find it warm out here, shall we go into the air-conditioning?'

'Not today.' He raised a barricading hand. 'You've woken me up, remember? And my number one priority is going back to bed.'

The scarlet mouth pouted in a flirty-flirty manner. Maybe the older woman considered she was milking her beauty for all it was worth, but in Clemence's opinion the pouty lips had much in common with a vacuum cleaner.

'You're refusing me permission to enter?'

'I am.'

Another Hoovering gesture was followed by acceptance in the form of a lift and fall of the green chiffon shoulders. Leyla turned to issue an instruction to the driver and, having made sure he had suitably banished himself inside the car, began to speak.

'I saw the two of you together last night. I saw you go into her bungalow.'

'Then it was you lurking—I thought so!' Jassim's voice gained an acid edge. 'And what gives you the right to spy on me?'

'You mean——?' Clemence gasped, as her brain-cells shuffled through the facts. Message understood, she switched astonished eyes from Jassim to the woman beneath the parasol and back again. 'You mean she's——'

His curt nod lodged the Mrs X in her throat.

'I was not spying. Because the creature had been involved both with Khalid and with you, it was clearly my duty to——' a phrase was sculptured '——to keep pace with events. Any other resourceful woman would have done the same,' Leyla informed him, too busy justifying herself to pay any attention to Clemence, let alone her surprise. On the contrary, despite being the object under discussion she was being studiously ignored. 'When I realised the girl seemed to be bewitching you—though heaven knows how or why—I decided to find out more about her. Yes, I followed you. And yes, I arranged with the switchboard to monitor her calls.'

'You did what?' demanded Jassim, biting into the last word.

'When Howard Harrell rang later, I listened in.'

'Give me strength!' he prayed, glancing towards heaven.

'I make no apologies.' His stepmother demonstrated a staggering aplomb. 'What I heard made interesting listening. For example, the fact that she had been unable to keep her husband satisfied came over loud and clear. Which means, Jassim, there's no chance whatsoever of her satisfying you.'

Clemence came out of shock. 'You have a nerve!' she snapped.

'It's time you got your facts straight, Leyla,' Jassim intruded, damming the torrent of protests she had waiting. He rubbed a palm across his naked chest and its mat of dark curly hair. 'For a start, Howard Harrell isn't Clemence's husband.'

The raven head was tilted to one side. 'Then you were aware that although they continued to call themselves Mr and Mrs, the marriage had already ended?'

'It hadn't ended, because——' he cast Clemence a glance as though seeking approval '—because it hadn't started. There was no marriage.'

Surprise restrained Leyla for a moment, then she bounced back like a malicious ball. 'The Harrell man had the sense not to shackle himself to a loser? He made sure he left himself a way out of their relationship? That doesn't surprise me in the least. He must have realised from the start she was—I believe an appropriate term would be a wrong 'un.'

'A wrong 'un!' squeaked Clemence.

'If anyone's wrong it's you, Leyla,' Jassim said grittily.

'You mentioned the likelihood that they could be splitting up,' his stepmother said, carrying on regardless. 'But have you any idea why?'

He closed weary eyes. 'I don't care why. I don't care to have you here. I don't care——'

'It's because another woman is carrying his child, and what's more——' Leyla paused, playing the scene as high drama '—Howard Harrell married that woman just a couple of day ago!'

'But he couldn't have done! I heard him . . . I thought . . .' The green eyes swung to her. 'Is this true, Clem?' he demanded.

'Er—yes,' she said, startled to find herself included.

He scoured his chest again. 'Oh, sunshine!'

'There's no need to feel sorry for her,' Leyla protested.

'No, there isn't.' Clemence found it odd to be in agreement. 'You see——'

'The man has ditched this creature and found someone new. It's clear he's head over heels about his "little love", as he calls her,' his stepmother intervened.

'I haven't been ditched.' Clemence hesitated. 'Well, yes, I suppose you could interpret it that way, but——' She hesitated again, a fatal mistake with Leyla around.

'Ditched, and yet the girl wishes them luck and tells him he's a great guy. How pathetic! What you should ask yourself, Jassim, is where's her pride, where's her backbone, where's her sense of worth?'

'It's not a matter of pride or worth,' Clemence started to object, but the parasol was waved so suggestively close to her head that the only sensible thing to do in the circumstances seemed to be to stand to one side and keep quiet. The woman was talking drivel anyway—she'd heard more sense from a puddle full of ducks—and, although she did not appreciate being maligned, allowing her to quack on seemed preferable to having an eye poked out.

'Howard Harrell intends to have nothing more to do with this ex-mistress of his once they've finished in Oman, and yet she grovels,' came the scornful continuation. 'Is that the kind of woman you want, Jassim?'

'I know the woman I *don't* want, Leyla,' Jassim said quietly. 'And that's you.'

'Me?' Leyla gasped.

'Clemence isn't worth tuppence, but you value yourself at a million dollars, isn't that what you came here to prove?'

A manicured hand dabbed at a stray curl. 'I don't need to prove anything. You and I——'

'There isn't a you and I. There never has been. There never will be. Because telling a woman to her face she doesn't appeal has always struck me as brutal, I've never laid it on the line. However, the way you've treated Clemence, this scene which you've staged, nullifies any finer feelings.' He hitched the pyjama trousers higher up his hips. 'Other men might drop around you like flies but, beautiful as you are, you leave me cold.'

Leyla bridled. 'No, I don't!'

'Sorry, you do. And it's not only any sexual rapport that's missing. To be honest, I can't think of one single way in which we're on the same wavelength.'

'We *are*. Jassim, you're an Arab like me and——'

'Half—but no matter what blood flows in my veins I was born and bred in Australia, and as far as I'm concerned that makes me an Australian. The longer I'm away from the place, the more I know it.'

'You have a good life here,' his stepmother protested. 'It could be even better.'

'If I shared it with you? No, thanks. Look, when I first came up with this pretence of being involved with Clemence, I hoped——'

'Pretence?' Leyla echoed.

'That's all it was at first.'

'And afterwards?' she demanded.

'Afterwards——' He shrugged. 'The point I'm getting at is that I hoped my attraction to a young woman who was a contemporary would open your eyes. I hoped you'd realise that if I was considering a partnership, it would be with someone like her, not you.'

'You don't like me because I'm dark while she's a blonde, or is it because I'm older?' The pale green bosom swelled. 'There's only eight years between us!'

'Age has nothing to do with it, nor the colour of your hair.'

'Then, in time, maybe——' She threw a hand outwards, the palm up like a successful conjurer.

'In time, nothing.' Frustration dynamited out of him. 'Face facts, Leyla, you and I are going nowhere. Hell, the only reason I appeal is because I remind you of my father!'

'No!'

'How often have you said we share similar traits?'

'But you do! He worked hard, like you. He was a strong personality, like you.'

'Not true, but even if certain parallels do exist I am not him.'

'I know.'

'Are you sure? Isn't it more the case that because he fell in love with you, you imagine I'll do the same? You almost consider it's my duty to do the same? It doesn't work that way. You can't use me to roll back the years to be young again and in love.'

'The idea of returning to my twenties does not excite me in the least,' Leyla retorted. 'Our friendship is——'

'Our friendship is a *family* friendship, no more,' Jassim said firmly. 'I was grateful for it in the past and if it continues into the future, which I trust it will, I shall be grateful then, too.'

After considering his statement for a moment, his stepmother swept the parasol from her shoulder and snapped it shut.

'I shall leave,' she declared, flouncing off towards the Mercedes.

She wrenched open the door and disappeared inside. An instant command was given to the driver.

'Hey, what about me?' appealed Clemence, when the engine thrummed to life.

'Leyla!' Jassim called. 'Don't forget you have a passenger.'

A window whirred down. 'You wanted her—you keep her!'

'Clemence needs to be returned to the Plaza,' he ordered, but the window slid up and the Mercedes moved forward. As it passed there was a glimpse of his stepmother sitting in the back, as aloof as a china pekinese. 'Leyla, wait!' In one bound Jassim was off the doorstep, across the porch and charging across the grass. 'Leyla, stop!' he pleaded, as the car reached the road. He leapt the low wall. 'You've no war to fight with Clemence. She and I are through.'

As the car gathered speed he flung a mouthful of obscenities and stood there, glaring until it turned a corner and disappeared.

'That woman!' he snarled, stomping back to the porch like a bad-tempered bear. 'She thrives on the grand gesture and to hell with the consequences!'

'There's no need to throw a fit just because she's left me here,' Clemence said tightly. She was not amused by his temper tantrum, not when it derived from the fact that she had been dumped on his doorstep like an unwanted package, a package which was becoming increasingly hot and sweaty. Maybe he didn't want her around, but there was no call for this aggression. 'I can return to the hotel by taxi,' she pointed out.

'Yes, you can. Oh!' He stared down at his foot. 'I've hurt myself.'

'If you will go running berserk without your shoes, what do you expect?'

'But there's blood!'

'Amazing.' She gave an indifferent shrug. 'You think Kickapoo Joy Juice should trickle out?'

Jassim made a close-eyed inspection. 'There's a deep cut,' he said, mortified. 'It must be at least an inch long.'

'You have a scratch which is half an inch, if that.'

'It needs to be bandaged.'

'And quickly, we can't allow you to bleed to death.' Clemence cast a disparaging glance. 'If you reckon a tourniquet's required I'll see what I can remember from First Aid class.'

He scowled. 'You're a regular dispenser of tea and sympathy!'

'And you're a regular softie. Now I recognise all that macho-stuff—the hat, the open-necked shirts, the jeep—for what it is—junk!'

To her surprise, Jassim grinned. 'Good, no more pretence. Shall I show you my embroidery?'

'I'd rather be shown a bandage, and a cool drink. One drink,' Clemence thought it wise to add, in case he reverted to objecting to her presence. 'Then perhaps you could telephone for a taxi? There is a phone here?'

'Yeah,' he said, and gestured for her to go indoors.

After giving his foot another inspection, he hobbled after her, wincing. They were winces which would not have disgraced someone who had had the misfortune to undergo major surgery on the day anaesthetic supplies ran dry.

Jassim had all the makings of a ham actor, Clemence decided. But weren't all men ham actors when injury was involved? She well remembered the time in Germany when Howard had broken his finger. His stuck-pig squeals had alerted half the hotel, and for weeks afterwards he had worn a martyred expression which had transcended all language barriers.

The hall Jassim had ushered her into, an airy place of whites and greens, was interestingly furnished. A Victorian chaise-longue, awash with mint-coloured cushions, sat before alcoves filled with books. Botanical prints hung on the walls, a Moroccan mother-of-pearl screen occupied the corner by the stairs, there was a huge globe set upon a mahogany stand. A collection of enamel eggs displayed on a hexagonal table gave notice of someone's appreciation of their jewel-bright beauty. Given the chance, Clemence would have loved to stop for a closer inspection.

'Whose house is this?' she enquired, as he led her from the hall into a bathroom opulent with sunken bath, gold fittings, mirrored walls which reflected an abundance of leafy plants.

'Mine.'

'Yours?'

'Mmm. I bought it last year. Should be a good investment.' Jassim opened a cabinet set into the tiled wall and frowned at the contents. 'The exterior was in good repair, but the interior required attention. I reckon the architect did a fine job.'

'He did. The house is lovely, but——' She began to falter.

'You're surprised I can afford it?' he finished for her, a grin twitching in the corner of his mouth.

'To be honest, yes.'

'We're in luck.' He produced a roll of bandage and a lint pad. 'You haven't exactly rushed to help, so perhaps I ought to fix my own wound?' he suggested, the grin taking on a hint of *cri de coeur*.

Clemence raised blue-grey eyes. 'Lord preserve me from helpless males!' she declared, and commandeered the bandage. 'Sit,' she instructed, pointing to the loo seat.

'Yeah, ma'am. Contrary to appearances, I am able to afford the occasional outlay of cash. This house was financed partly with money earned here and partly with funds brought in from Australia,' he revealed, as she dampened a face flannel and knelt down to clean his foot. 'I own a trucking business back there. Tom, that's my mother's second husband, is currently running things on my behalf. And running them well. Profits last quarter hit an all-time high.'

'But why leave a flourishing concern behind in order to come and work in Oman as a mechanic?' Clemence enquired, blonde head bent as she concentrated on her task. It was fortunate they had something to talk about, because touching him—even an action as prosaic as bathing his foot—had revived memories of the awesome intimacy they had once shared. She knew her pulse-rate had increased. And if they hadn't been talking, then perhaps he would have detected the annoying tremble of her fingers.

'I'm not *just* a mechanic, though that's how I started off fifteen or so years ago.' Jassim gave a shamefaced grin. 'I own the company here, too. The fleet of concrete-mixers belongs to me.'

'You? But the house in the desert is so basic that I thought——' She broke off. 'You mentioned your boss, but you took damn good care not to let me know it was you!' she accused.

'I prefer not to advertise my wealth.'

'You didn't.' She glared at his foot, transferring the feeling of awesome intimacy into annoyance. 'This ought to be washed with antiseptic. Got any?'

'In the cabinet, and don't be cross. OK, so I glossed over my assets, but the reason I've been less than honest is that a couple of years ago I suffered a bad experience. One which made me determined that in future I'd make sure I was appreciated for myself and not my bank account. Ouch!' he protested when she dabbed on the antiseptic. 'It stings!'

'Tough!'

'Clem, you can't imagine what a relief it was to know you didn't care——' he snapped his fingers '—that much about my financial status. Not like Roz,' he added pungently.

'Oh, Roz. I saw her name in one of your books,' said Clemence, when he cast a questioning look.

'The book which, among other things, featured rich oil princes,' Jassim said drily. 'It was supposed to encourage me to take more of an interest in the Arabic side of my family.'

'And did it?'

'Oddly enough, yes—though it was the historical angle which intrigued, not the princes. Roz was always harping on about how I should get to grips with my roots, but up until then I hadn't done much about it. I suppose that book changed my life, in so much as it influenced my decision to come to Oman.' He bent forward. 'Is the cut very deep?'

'Not as serious as you imagined, but worse than I thought. However, the bleeding's stopped, so with luck you should live.'

'Gee, thanks. Roz was the bad experience. Want to hear about her?'

'If you want to tell me,' Clemence replied. She had intended to sound offhand, but knew her tone had been irritated. This hand/foot contact had an odd effect. Even Jassim seemed at odds, keen to talk where minutes ago he had been set on her departure.

'I met her around four years ago. Up to that point the

truck company had superseded everything, so although a
series of women had passed through my life whenever any
of them had started pushing for a commitment I'd waved a
hasty goodbye. Then came Roz.' Jassim sniffed. 'She
worked in advertising, was doing well in her own right, and
seemed unimpressed by my growing affluence. If you have
an Arab name, there's a tendency for people to imagine you
must be rolling in the dough. Some edge closer for that one
reason,' he added as a cryptic aside.

'You're always on the alert against them?' Clemence
suggested.

He frowned. 'Could be.'

'You are. Grief, all I needed to do was say "Have a nice
day" to Khalid and you started taking pot shots!'

'I'll do my best to curb the instinct in future,' he promised
with a smile, then returned to being serious. 'My
relationship with Roz developed, and after a while I
suggested she move in with me.'

Clemence began unwinding the bandage. 'Why didn't
you go straight ahead and marry her?'

'Don't know. I've often wondered about that myself.' A
cloud passed over his face. 'Maybe, like Howard with you,
some instinct warned that our relationship might not last.'

'Jassim, Howard and I——'

'The instinct was totally subconscious.'

'Jass——'

'Roz and I had been living together for eighteen months
or so,' he continued, sturdily denying her the right to speak,
'when she suggested we legalise the situation. I agreed. A
date was chosen, the guests invited, then——' He sighed.
'About three weeks before the ceremony I was at a pre-
wedding bash which a group of her colleagues from work
had organised. I arrived at the restaurant on time, but Roz
had got tied up with a client. While we were waiting for her
one of the fellows, the office blabbermouth, made a crack

about Roz landing a rich guy who looked like being even richer. I asked what he meant. He hedged, but eventually admitted that Roz had been spreading the word that when my father died, I stood to gain. At the time my father had undergone a second operation for stomach cancer and his prospects weren't good.'

Clemence placed the pad over the cut and wrapped the bandage around. 'You didn't gain,' she pointed out. 'Khalid inherited the Plaza.'

'Yeah, but my father remembered me in his will even though we hadn't set eyes on each other for nearly thirty years. Bear with me, I'll tell you about that in a minute. To say it hurt when I found money *did* matter where Roz's feelings for me were concerned was an understatement,' Jassim continued, his eyes bleak with remembered pain. 'That evening was the longest in my life. The minute I could I drove her home, where I told her point blank I didn't expect to receive anything from my father.' He sliced a hand through the air. 'Not a bean.'

'So where had she got the idea that you'd benefit?'

'It seems she'd combined bits I'd told her about my background, with information from a school pal of mine. The guy had given her a grossly exaggerated tale of my father's wealth which had raised great expectations. Roz had begun to anticipate, to gloat.' The green eyes were glacial. 'You should have seen her face when I revealed that I'd never make millionaire! And that I didn't particularly *want* to make millionaire. I'm ambitious, yes. But it's the satisfaction of achievement which matters to me, not acquiring a mountain-high pile of cash.' He made an impatient gesture. 'If I'd wanted confirmation that all she registered when she looked at me were dollar signs, I had it then.'

'Jass, you're hardly the Hunchback of Notre Dame,' Clemence protested. 'Money can't have been her sole motivation for liking you, for——' the word lodged like a bone in her throat '—loving you.'

'As far as she was concerned, it represented the lynchpin of our relationship.'

'Then the girl must have been crazy!'

Clemence grabbed the scissors she had found in the medicine cabinet and cut down the middle of the loose length of bandage. Kneeling, she bound the two ends around his foot and tied them in a knot. When her task was accomplished, she lapsed into thoughts of Jassim and love, but found them too disturbing. As a diversion, she raised her head and gave an impudent smile.

'What's the lynchpin of your relationship with your stepmother? Your body?'

'Push off!' he growled.

'That's not very polite.'

He grinned, relaxing. 'Clem, it's as polite as I can make it. I'd phrase it very differently if it weren't for the fact that I'm a gentleman.'

'It must flatter a gentleman's ego to have his beautiful stepmother lusting after him,' she teased.

'Flatter? Flatten, more like.' Jassim pulled a face. 'Having a middle-aged woman playing coy is bloody embarrassing.'

She giggled. 'Leyla gives the word "determined" a whole new meaning. Can you put your hand over your heart and swear she's never manoeuvred you into a corner and had her demon way with you?'

'If she had got me in a corner it wouldn't be my heart I'd have needed to put my hand over,' he remarked drolly, 'but to answer your question—I always managed to escape.'

Clemence laughed. 'There was a fellow human being reaching out, and yet you said no? How could you?'

'With the greatest of ease.'

'Presumably embarrassment was the reason you kept

quiet about the identity of——' she quoted like a beldame of the theatre '—the mysterious Mrs X?'

'It was, with the added reason that when I first thought up the idea I wasn't exactly sure where I stood with you. At the time discretion seemed the better part of valour, or something along those lines.' Jassim appraised the bandage. 'Looks fine.'

'Thanks. Want to give it a trial to check that I've not cut off a vital artery or something? Maybe I ought to pop round to the local hospital and ask to borrow a pair of crutches?' Clemence suggested, when he rose and took a couple of careful steps.

'Maybe you ought to shut up.'

Unrepentant, she grinned. 'If you wore slippers it'd keep the bandage in place and clean.'

'I'll find a pair in a minute.' He reached down to where she knelt. 'Come on, you deserve that drink.'

She hesitated. Once before he had held out a tanned hand and subsequently held her in his arms. But he wasn't going to hold her in his arms now. Not now, when he had yelled at Leyla that the two of them were through. And sounded as though he meant it. If there had been a way of refusing his offer Clemence would have done so, instead she linked her hand with his. His touch revived more memories—how his fingers had entwined themselves in her hair, how he had stroked her breasts. On her feet, she broke contact and walked quickly ahead out into the hall. Last night she had attributed his 'no future' comment to a lack of finance, but that was not the case. And even if his confusion pointed to him having misconstrued the phone call with Howard—his line-tapping stepmother had clarified that little matter! Clemence sighed. His insistence that they were through clashed dramatically with the insistent desire she felt for him, and made a hasty departure imperative.

'Forget the drink,' she told him. 'Just find me a taxi.'

'No need. I'll drive you back to the hotel.'

'How? Press on the brake pedal and you'll put pressure on your foot. Chances are the cut'll open up, and start bleeding again, and——' She zigzagged a hand. 'I can't allow you to take me back in the jeep.'

'I wouldn't be. I also run a BMW—with a feather-touch brake pedal.' Jassim grinned at her from beneath his lashes. 'Are you impressed?'

'Incredibly,' she said, and he laughed.

'I've still to tell you about the inheritance I received from my father. Why not have a drink while you listen, and then we'll sort out the transport?'

'I understood you were tired and only interested in going back to bed.'

'You think I can sleep after all that's been happening here today?' He limped to the end of the hall and opened double doors. 'If you're not desperate for a drink, I am.'

When he smiled and his dimple appeared, Clemence could not resist. She walked forward, but on the threshold of the room, she paused. Jassim had opened the door on to a light and spacious lounge. One wall, built entirely of sliding glass panels, looked out on to a garden where palm trees shaded a lawn studded with bushes of pink hibiscus and white bougainvillaea. The view was impressive, but her eyes travelled beyond it to the far wall. Here an outcrop of silver-grey granite protruded into the room, and over the rock ferns and blossoms tumbled in glorious disarray. This feature was spectacular.

'Both my Omani houses are adjacent to mountains,' Jassim told her, pleased by her admiration. 'But in this case the mountain is built in. Grooves cut into the rock have been filled with soil, so everything you see is growing in situ.' He gestured across acres of honey-coloured carpet to a white leather sofa and chairs. 'What would you like to drink? I can offer more than bottled water this time. How about some wine?'

'Please, with lots of ice.'

'Two minutes,' he said, and disappeared.

The lounge, like the hall, contained much to intrigue. The wall surrounding an antique writing-desk had been pinned with black and white sketches of Oman, and Clemence was studying these when he returned.

'The wounded soldier's reduced to fetching and carrying for himself?' she smiled, as he set down a tray bearing a bottle of wine, ice bucket and two glasses. 'What's happened to Sunthi?'

'It's his day off. And I miss him. I'll miss him even more when I return to Australia.'

'When's that?'

'In another six months.'

'For good?'

'Brisbane will be my permanent base, but I intend to visit Oman from time to time to keep an eye on things.' Jassim poured the wine and added ice-cubes. He passed her a brimming glass. 'That is, unless Leyla decides to bear a grudge and has me banned as an undesirable alien!'

Clemence laughed. 'Didn't you say she screams a lot but rarely follows through? My guess is once she's got over her pique, she'll transfer her affections to some other blockhead.'

'Blockhead?'

'You must admit that the smart thing, the moment you realised she wanted more than a platonic relationship, would have been to make it plain then and there that it was no go.'

'I do, but I'm not that smart.' Jassim took a mouthful of wine. 'I was going to tell you about my inheritance.'

'Changing the subject?'

'If you mean am I avoiding an in-depth discussion of my

inadequacies? Yes, like the plague. Remember I said the Al Foris were not pleased when my father married my mother?' Clemence nodded. 'Well, through a mixture of threats, blackmail and sheer hostile pressure in time they persuaded him to divorce her. I was three when he returned to Oman. Despite the divorce he promised he'd come back and see us, but he never did. The family wouldn't allow it. I know Leyla portrays my father as having a will of his own, but that's to boost her self-esteem. Can you imagine a marriage between her and anyone resilient? God Almighty, it'd be a fight to the death! No, he was weak. I know that from what my mother's told me, from the way he caved in over the divorce, from his letters.'

'Your father wrote?'

'He channelled correspondence through an old uncle here. The uncle didn't approve, but my father managed to persuade him he was entitled to news about his eldest son. It was done on the sly—had to be, because the family regarded my mother and me as forbidden topics.'

'He never protested?'

'Didn't have the courage. Still, there's one thing in his favour, despite a never-ending procession of nubile young girls being brought to his attention, nine years passed before he took a second bride. Ironical, because my mother married Tom in less than three.'

'So your father genuinely cared, and yet allowed himself to be stampeded away?' Clemence said. 'That's sad.'

Jassim nodded. 'During the latter period of his life he was sick and contact dwindled, but his will proved how deep his feelings had been. My mother received a healthy sum of cash, while my legacy consisted of a quarry, parcels of land, plus a collection of defunct concrete-mixers. My father may have been a dead loss where sticking up for himself was concerned, yet businesswise he couldn't be beaten. He was a mixture of entrepreneur and magpie, making money from buying and selling land, mineral rights, warehouses, anything that promised to show a profit. The bulk of what he'd amassed had been cashed in to finance the hotel—the Plaza was built at Leyla's insistence, with Khalid in mind—but he'd salted away enough to leave me and my mother something worthwhile.'

'What did Leyla think about that?' she asked curiously.

He gave a wry smile. 'Despite having achieved what she desired—her boy child falling heir as specified—she was hopping mad, like the rest of the Al Foris. When my uncle notified us of my father's death I wrote to her, but she didn't reply. It seems Leyla was all for keeping my mother and me in the dark about the bequests, but the old uncle insisted we should be informed. My father had died a few months after I'd split with Roz, so I decided to visit Oman.'

Clemence sipped her wine. 'Because you wanted to come, or because you wanted to get away?' she queried.

'A bit of both. From a distance the inheritance, pleasing though it was, didn't appear to be any big deal. But having something else to think about other than Roz was a relief, and therapeutic. Tom offered to fill in, so I came.'

'Not intending to stay for two and a half years?'

'No,' Jassim said, and grinned. 'I was in a bloody-minded frame of mind, and spending three or four weeks in Oman while I laid claim to my land, etcetera, seemed a neat way of thumbing my nose at the Al Foris. But when I examined what I'd been left I realised it wasn't peanuts, after all. I sold most of the land, but when I disposed of the quarry I did a deal with the new owner. Due to a sudden take-off in the Omani economy, his products were in high demand and the guy had severe transport problems,' he explained. 'I suggested I assist with the ready-mixed concrete side of his business. The air here is hot and dry, so although at first glance the mixers I'd inherited looked worthless, the engines simply needed to be greased, a few adjustments made, and—boom, boom—they were functioning again. I started up the depot and——'

'All this couldn't have happened in one month,' Clemence interrupted.

'It didn't. I'm getting ahead of myself. When I realised my father had left me—I suppose "potential" is the best word, I couldn't bear to see it go to waste. I travelled home to Brisbane, bored Tom stiff talking about what a challenge it would be to get a business here off the ground and, I suspect to shut me up as much as anything, he offered to mind the store. He'd been in from the early days, so he knew what to do. Tom's a great guy,' Jassim said affectionately. 'Also by that time I'd become interested in exploring the Arab side of me, and he understood.'

'Have you explored it?'

'Yes.'

'And?'

'And like I told Leyla, I feel more Australian than a goddamn koala!'

'How come you speak such good Arabic?' Clemence enquired, holding out her glass as he offered a refill of wine.

'I don't.' His dimple shone. 'To be truthful, I speak it with a strong Queensland lilt. But I learnt the language as a kid. The only time my father ever came near to insisting on anything was a request that I attend classes. I went for a while, but as I grew older the beach tugged. I derived more of a kick from riding surf than making vowel sounds! However, when I took a brush-up course before coming out here much of what I'd learned came back to me.'

Clemence looked at him across the rim of the cut-crystal wine-glass. 'About Leyla,' she said. 'She didn't want you here and yet now she's enamoured; what happened, did she take one look and keel over?'

'Nothing so instant, though she did accept me far quicker than any other member of the Al Fori tribe. At our first meeting my resemblance to my father appeared to knock her back a bit—photographs of him when he was young could be photographs of me—and our similarity also tended to confuse everyone else. It was easy to distance themselves from a half-caste Aussie and turn him into a bogeyman, but seeing me in the flesh, Al Fori flesh, altered perspectives.'

'Now you're accepted?'

'More or less, but not just because of the way I look,' Jassim stressed. 'What really changed things, first with Leyla and eventually with the rest of the family, was when they realised I didn't represent a threat.'

Clemence frowned. 'Why should you?'

'It seems they were afraid that, as the eldest son, I'd lay claim to *all* my father's possessions, namely the Plaza. They're proud of the hotel, and justifiably. It's a symbol of the Al Foris' standing in the community. Visions of me ordering lawyers to grab control, only to sell it and board the next Qantas flight with the profits tucked in my hip pocket, had built up a nasty head of steam. It was a long time before they accepted that I had no hankerings in that direction, but once they were convinced it made all the difference.'

'Like Leyla installing you as her dream hero?'

He mouthed something coarse.

Clemence laughed. 'I thought you were a gentleman?'

'Only twenty-three hours a day.'

'Is someone lined up to mind the store here when you return to Australia?'

'Yeah, though it won't be minding so much as taking charge. From the start the intention was for locals to run the show, so personnel have been trained along the way. A couple of Omani graduates head the company as business manager and accountant.'

'And having employed people to cover those areas, the

managing director's free to spend his time mending broken down trucks?' she enquired pertly.

'OK, I have this habit of throwing myself into the nitty-gritty when I could be pushing paper around, but fixing engines is fun. Except on Fridays.'

'Fun, but dirty work. Ye gods, the first time I saw you I though what a sight you looked!' Clemence laughed.

'Don't you start! I get enough hassle from Sunthi. When I arrive home at night, he's waiting at the door like a ravening Dobermann to order me to change. He has a special chainsaw voice he keeps for the occasion. Whenever he talks about the house in the desert, he uses his chainsaw voice, too.'

'I'm not surprised. The pool apart, that place could do double duty as a punishment block.'

'It serves its purpose,' Jassim protested. 'You see, when I started up the depot I worked even longer hours than I do now, which meant I needed a base close at hand. The house was conveniently located and cheap, so I bought it as somewhere to lay my head, nothing more. That's why I've never bothered much about comfort. These days I live here and rarely use it. I only took you there on the spur of the moment.' He had a drink of wine. 'If you'd known what was happening that night you'd have realised I spent a good half-hour on the doctor's telephone, talking to Sunthi. I needed to arrange for him to be driven out from Muscat, together with food supplies. When he realised I intended taking you there, he accused me of being out of my head.' He stared down into his glass. 'I think perhaps I was.'

'But you took me to give yourself a let-out with Leyla.'

'Did I? Yeah. Whoopee. Yeah, I took you because of Leyla. Yeah, maybe I also took you because there seemed a chance, a tiny one, that you might still kick up and report Khalid to the police. But the main reason why I took you was that——'

'What?' Clemence asked, when he dried up.

'Because I wanted you near me.' Jassim fixed his green eyes on a far horizon. 'It sounds so corny, and I know it doesn't make much sense considering how up until then we'd been engaged in a more or less perpetual battle, but I needed you around. You, not any other woman. I needed to look at you, to absorb the essence of you. I needed you sleeping under my roof, in my house, because—because that would make it seem as though you belonged. Belonged to me.' He gave a cracked kind of laugh. 'They say the more a man blusters, the more afraid he is of being found out, and that's what I was doing that night. It was as though I'd fallen into those quicksands I told you about, and was thrashing this way and that. I know I reckoned that when I undressed you and put you in my shirt it made no impression, but I lied. I was a quivering mass, Clem. I *shook*! There were all kinds of problems with the buttons because my fingers were shaking so much. God Almighty, you do things to me Roz never did!' He raised his head and flung her a bruiser of a look, then continued quickly, 'I must also have been out of my head to allow matters to reach a state where Leyla needed a confrontation. The way she spoke to you today——'

'It's over,' Clemence insisted.

He took no notice. 'The truth is I dreaded one of her scenes, so in the past I chickened out.' He gulped down the dregs of his wine. 'Clem,' he said earnestly, 'I realise those things she said about you must have hurt, but take no notice. She might belittle you for still loving the fellow even though he's gone off and married someone else, but I don't. I know feelings aren't something you can control. Love can't be turned on and off, like a light switch.' He reached across to run the back of his finger along her wrist in a brief, comforting touch. 'I understand.'

'No, you don't. To begin with, I don't love Howard.'

He sighed. 'You might try and tell yourself that, but it isn't true. Like it or not, the guy's an integral part of your life.'

'Jass, listen——'

'Sunshine, I heard you talking to him on the telephone. I know a bond exists.'

'You know nothing!' Clemence's wine-glass went down with a clatter on a side table. 'Yes, there's a bond, and there always will be. But only because Howard Harrell is my *cousin*.'

CHAPTER NINE

'YOUR cousin?' Jassim said cautiously.

'Yes!'

'You don't——'

'No!'

There was a long pause.

'You realise when he spoke to you on the phone, I thought he was asking you to marry him? And I thought you said yes.'

'I realise you thought wrong,' returned Clemence.

'And that after Leyla put me straight, it made no difference because I was convinced you were pining for him? Convinced you were so emotionally tied up with Howard there was no hope of me ever——' He rubbed at his brow. 'I know you were supposed to have finished with the guy, yet I detected a reluctance to accept a final break.'

'How could I make a final break? Even if I wasn't to see him again, a cousin is a cousin is a cousin, for evermore.'

Another pause followed.

'You could have told me Howard was no more, no less than a bloody relation,' grumbled Jassim.

'I tried, but every time I started you shut me up. Jass, do you think if I loved someone I'd let him go without putting up a fight? I do possess a shade more oomph than that!'

He frowned. 'It did seem strange how there were no recriminations, no bitterness,' he admitted, 'but I thought you were being . . . noble.'

'Like I was noble in the bungalow last night with you?'

Clemence enquired, the momentum of the moment carrying her into an area she had previously decided was best ignored.

'That could have been attributed to a sudden fit of lust,' he muttered.

'Lust!' She gave a strangled laugh. 'Did lust motivate you?'

'No. No, I——' He hesitated, and when he spoke again it was to go off at a tangent. 'If it wasn't to cover up an affair for the sake of convention, why do—why *did* you and Howard pass yourselves off as man and wife?'

'To deter the attentions of the less savoury element of the male population. When Harrell & Co started up my father had made it plain to Howard that he'd prefer me to be chaste with a t, rather than chased with a d, and Howard doesn't take his responsibilities lightly.'

'It didn't work with Khalid,' he commented.

'The system isn't foolproof, though it does eliminate the majority of what used to be called stage door johnnies. Because of show-business being a glamour industry, the girls involved are often expected to be—open to suggestion,' Clemence explained. 'Dancers, singers, the back end of the pantomime donkey, you name it, we all get our share of hassle.'

Jassim cast her a glance. 'I imagine you come in for a larger share than most.'

She shrugged. 'What happened was that when we first hit the road, our bookings included a spell at a nightclub managed by a man called Ralph.'

'To sidetrack, why did you and Howard choose to hit the road in the first place?'

'The road chose us. You see, when we were students——'

'Students where?'

'The Royal College of Music.'

'Highbrow stuff,' Jassim commented.

'Are you impressed?'

He grinned. 'Incredibly.'

'We come from a family of musicians,' Clemence continued. 'My father's the leader of a symphony orchestra, my mother plays the cello. Howard's parents take care of the woodwind side. As we'd been steeped in music from being——' she held out a hand '—this big, it was taken for granted we'd do something in that line. But classical. As student grants come on the lean side, we teamed up at college and began playing popular music in pubs in our spare time. The idea was simply to make money. Our act went down well. We were punctual, always properly rehearsed, so we gained a reputation for reliability.'

'And for being easy on the eye.'

'Maybe. The end result was an approach from an agent when we graduated. Bernie guaranteed a series of bookings, some in clubs but mostly on the international hotel circuit. The money he quoted was far more than we could ever have hoped to bring in from orchestral work. Neither set of parents was thrilled when we decided to give it a spin, but they had to admit it'd be foolish to turn down a solid offer of employment.' Clemence sighed. 'Ralph was good looking, smooth, slick with the patter, and despite the fact that he must have used half a pint of aftershave a day, I fell with a thud. I was young and gullible, and it never struck me that we had only one thing in common—we were both in love with him.' She pulled down her mouth, mocking the dedication she had once felt. 'When he spoke of making me his bride, I believed him. I floated around with my head in the clouds, until one day a member of the nightclub staff decided he'd better have a word.'

'And?' Jassim prompted, when she hesitated.

'It transpired Ralph had dated a good seventy-five per cent of the girls who had appeared at the club, and that each romance had ended the moment their gig ended. When I confronted him, he confesssed I wasn't going to be the exception. Because he's one of nature's St Bernard's, my cousin forced a slug of brandy down my throat and dragged me out of the snow, then thought up the idea of us pretending to be married.'

'Apart from Khalid it's been effective?'

'We came across an ultra-determined Italian once, but on the whole—yes.'

'Are you telling me there's been no one since Ralph?'

Clemence smiled. 'No. I've had the normal quota of contacts with the opposite sex, though with us always on the move there hasn't been much chance of sustaining a relationship. For the past four years Howard can rightfully claim the position of *the* man in my life.'

Jassim's brow furrowed. 'Haven't the pair of you taken things a bit far? I mean, sharing accommodation?'

'That hasn't happened before,' she assured him quickly. 'Prior to our coming the Plaza sent details of the bungalow where we'd be staying, so we knew in advance there were beds available in separate rooms. If there hadn't been, I don't know what we'd have done.' She shrugged. 'The man-and-wife tag was for public consumption only. Every place else we've worked the management knew we were Mr and *Miss* Harrell and allotted accommodation accordingly. If anyone had taken the trouble to look behind the façade, they'd have realised that as married couples went we were distinctly odd.'

'I did.' Jassim agreed laconically. 'When Howard rushed off hotfoot, as you know, I suspected there might be another woman, but I also wondered if his leaving you alone here could be part of some grander strategy.'

'Such as?'

'I toyed with the idea of his deliberately exiting in order to leave the field clear for you to——'

'Fraternise with gentlemen in bars?' Clemence inserted crisply. 'You have a nasty, suspicious mind!'

'I question things that don't seem right. It's healthy,' he protested. 'Hell, how was I to know Howard was leaving because he wanted to fraternise with a woman at the altar?'

'He didn't, then. It was Yvonne raising fears that she could be having a miscarriage which enticed him home. Though her so-called twinges turned out to be a load of baloney, as I suspected! But with Howard back in residence, she was able to use her womanly wiles to persuade him to take a trip down the aisle.'

'You don't like Yvonne?' enquired Jassim, straightfaced.

'How did you guess?'

'The cracking of your knuckles was a dead giveaway.'

'I accept that she has every right to expect him to marry her and that he wants to, what I find objectionable is the underhand way she's gone about the entire affair.' Clemence frowned. 'Yvonne thrives on being simpering and submissive, but it's all an act geared to getting her own way.'

'Tell me about her,' he invited.

'She worked in the office at the music college. She must have seen Howard and decided he was Mr Wonderful, because most days she appeared to be lurking around every corner he turned, fluttering her lashes and rolling goo-goo eyes.'

'What was his reaction?'

'None. He barely seemed to notice her. In time Yvonne

moved up a gear. She muscled into our group, wangled invitations to parties, and generally made herself a nuisance. When Howard still paid no attention she enlisted me to promote her cause.' Clemence shook her head in wonderment. 'I told her my influence where my cousin's choice of women was concerned was nil, but she wouldn't believe me. Then, when he became interested in a close friend of mine, she stopped me in the corridor one day. With tears glistening, she accused me of pushing my friend forward and turning Howard against her. It was rubbish and I said so, but—oh heavens, it was dreadful!—her bottom lip quivered and the sobs started. The only way I could think of to comfort her was to promise to help, and—click—the tears stopped. But when she accosted me the next week and went through the same routine, and the week after that, it was too much. Her use of emotional blackmail, the way she tried to manipulate, got a long way up my nose.'

'Did you attempt to interest Howard in her?'

'I'd explained that Yvonne liked him, though I hadn't revealed the pressure she was applying because that would have made him run a mile. In retrospect,' she said drily, 'I rather wish I had done.'

'Then she wouldn't have ended up as your—what, cousin-in-law?' grinned Jassim. 'What happened next?'

'When Howard continued to date my friend, Yvonne became very cool towards me.'

'And vice versa?'

'I had no axe to grind, but——' Clemence shrugged. 'Call it clash of personalities or whatever, she is not my favourite person. We left college and, as I thought and hoped and prayed, left Yvonne behind us for ever, but about a year ago we were engaged to appear in a hotel in

Albufeira on the Algarve. We walked in through the revolving doors and who should we see standing in front of an advance poster of Harrell & Co but Miss Waterworks herself! Once again she made goo-goo eyes, only this time Howard did take note.'

'Was she smug?' he asked.

'Incredibly, and you needn't laugh.'

'Me, laugh?' Jassim protested, all innocence.

'It's thanks to Yvonne I was left to moulder here, and it's also due to her I'll be out of a job in a month's time. I don't consider that hilarious.'

He edged nearer across the sofa. 'I disagree.' His smile was warm and engaging. 'It seems to me Yvonne is not so much a pain in the rear as a fairy godmother—*my* fairy godmother.'

He was sitting close, so close that the mosquito which had buzzed since he had first opened the front door began making clarion calls. Could he hear the mosquito? Clemence wondered. He must. Weren't his green eyes wandering over her face in a way which hinted that it was not only her pulse-rate which had increased?

'How do you work that out?' she asked, a trifle short of breath.

'Easy. If she hadn't removed Howard, you wouldn't have been left here alone. If you hadn't been left alone, I wouldn't have begun my daily patrols and fallen in love with you. And as far as you soon being out of a job's concerned, I applaud her.'

He loved her! He loved her! Much as Clemence longed to fling her arms around his neck, smother him in kisses, and blubber that she loved him, too—she didn't. Having so often scoffed at Yvonne's on-tap tears, and being desperate to know what came next, she made herself stay cool.

'Applaud?' she enquired with care. 'Why would you applaud her?'

'I assume you were intending to instruct your agent to find you work, or maybe even hawk yourself around to see if someone would take you on?'

'Um—yes.'

'No need. I know a man who'll do just that, though he'll require some special clauses to be inserted into your contract.'

'What kind of clauses?' she asked cautiously.

'Guarantees that you won't go throwing yourself out of jeeps ever again, and that if you embark on a long walk he gets to go with you.' An arm came around her shoulders. 'But the most important clause stipulates that you love, honour and obey.' She received an amused glance. 'On second thoughts, maybe I should replace "obey" with "agree with occasionally".'

A warm glow infused her. '*You* should replace?' Clemence enquired, happily playing along with the game. 'So you'd be willing to take me on?'

'A long-term booking, like for the rest of your life. Will you marry me?'

'Yes, please,' she said, straight from the heart. Then her head took over. 'But we've only known each other a month.'

Jassim smiled. 'Do I feel like a stranger to you.'

'No. It's as though we've known each other for years. Hundreds of years. Thousands of years.'

'Ditto. Perhaps we were lovers in a previous life.'

'We must have been,' she agreed, gazing into his eyes. The arm around her shoulders tightened.

'Clem, I love you.'

'And I love you.'

Whether she smothered him in kisses or whether Jassim smothered her was a moot point, but there were endless kisses, and when they found the time to speak coherently again, Clemence lay half beneath him. With her corn-coloured hair spread across the cushion, with her bright eyes, with her mouth a little swollen and lips slightly parted, she had the soft, tumbled look of a woman made for love and for loving.

'There's another clause,' said Jassim, sliding his hand under her tee-shirt to caress the silky skin of her midriff.

'Now you tell me,' she murmured.

'There's to be a nightly performance in my bed.'

'Is performance the right word?' she enquiring, smiling up at him. 'Shouldn't it be appearance?'

His hand reached her breast, his fingers spreading to claim and fondle the full rounded curve with its pert pinnacle.

'My darling, for the first year at least we'll stick with performance. OK?'

Clemence did not get to answer, for he kissed her long and deep, and when he eventually drew back and smiled into her eyes, she was making no sense at all.

'It's to be twice nightly,' Jassim decided, like a lawyer adding a codicil.

'Whatever you want,' she murmured.

'I want to go to bed. Now.'

'I thought you reckoned you wouldn't be able to sleep?' Clemence replied dreamily.

'I won't.' He raised himself from her and from the sofa and bent to take hold of her two hands. 'Come on,' he grinned. 'I've been injured, remember? I need someone beautiful to lean on.'

For one of the walking wounded, Jassim managed to

climb the stairs in a remarkably short time, despite stopping to kiss his assistant on the way. Along a broad landing he steered them into a cool and serene bedroom where the walls were white with a bluebell tinge, and polished rosewood furniture sat on a rich cerulean carpet. The wide windows, which gave a glimpse of the palms in the garden, were curtained in white muslin and pale blue brocade with a silky thread. On a king-sized bed, a matching coverlet had been thrown askew. The bed was their destination. At it, Jassim stopped. Slowly, lingeringly, sensually, his eyes rolled down from her face to her throat, to where the tight peaks of her breasts were lifting the shirt's yellow cotton.

'I love you,' he said again. 'I want you.' He raised a finger to nudge first one rigid nipple and then the other. 'And you want me.'

'I do,' she agreed, and as the nudging became a touch, a stroking, a caress, it was difficult to stand.

Jassim caught hold of her hand and held it to his chest. 'Feel how my heart's beating? Feel the throb?' He propelled her fingers over the rough black furze of body hair and down across the muscled plane of his stomach to his thighs. 'Feel what effect you have on me?'

A bolt of electricity rocked her, and she sighed, her body moulding to his. Their mouths met again as Jassim bore her down beneath him on to the bed.

'I want you naked,' he muttered, his kisses trailing a heated path from her mouth to her throat to her shoulder. Needing access to the silken swell of her breasts, he pushed the shirt aside. 'Naked, *now*,' he insisted, and caught hold of the shirt's lower hem to peel it off over her head in one fluid movement. With equal speed, her other clothes were dispensed with.

Green eyes dark and smoky with desire, Jassim bent to run his tongue around the perfect peak of one golden breast, and Clemence gave a gasp of delight. An ache was growing, an ache which insisted he must be naked, too. She wanted desperately to feel the press of his warm smooth flesh against hers, to explore every bulge of muscle, every part of him. Her hand on his hip was all the message he needed. He ripped away the pyjama trousers, and then they were together. Golden skin met skin of honey. He bent his head, his dark hair brushing her shoulder as he kissed her breasts. Hot colours flashed and rotated in her head, until she moaned out loud.

'Love me, Jass. Love me,' she begged, lost in the caress of his mouth, his tongue, his fingers.

'Please,' he teased tenderly.

'Please. Please. Please!'

With masterful dedication he did as she requested, until ecstasy claimed her. She had never known anything so all-consuming, so complete. Limbs entwined, torso against torso, fevered mouth meeting mouth, they moved together. A fire burned, fusing their bodies to one.

'Please,' Clemence whimpered. '*Now.*'

'Yes,' Jassim said huskily. 'Oh, my darling. Yes!'

He took control, leading her up and up and up to a climax which came as a giddying explosion, one which probed deep to the core, splitting her apart into a thousand delirious fragments.

Outside a hot breeze stirred amongst the palm trees. The sun shifted from its noon position to slide down the sky. Time passed; lazy, contented time. A time when words of love were whispered, and lips met in languid kisses, and plans were idly made. Then a stray tanned finger moved, muscles stirred again, the fuse was relit. Ardent of mouth and gentle of touch, Jassim devoted himself to the worship of her body. If the first time urgent passion had brought them together, now love held sway, deep and flowing and strong. All the poetry and passion Clemence had ever yearned for lived in his kisses, gilded his caress. She wanted to laugh, she wanted to cry. She did both, holding his dark head to her breast. He entered her. Her body clenched, receiving his until she did not know where she ended and be began. Another whimper. Another husky sound from deep within his chest. And ... bliss.

'Maybe sleeping does seem like a good idea, after all.' Jassim murmured, as they lay drained and replete in each other's arms. 'For ten minutes at least.'

On the point of agreement, Clemence took hold of his wrist and inspected the watch he wore there. One look, and her blue-grey eyes shot open.

'It's four o'clock!' she exclaimed. She pushed herself from him. 'Jass, I'm sorry, but I have to go. I must. I'm due on stage at the Plaza at six. It'll take me at least an hour to get back there, then I need to shower and shampoo my hair, and——'

He sat up against the pillow. 'We could phone Otto and ask him to rustle up the Indians,' he suggested.

Clemence frowned. 'It's an idea.'

'You don't like it?'

'No. Although I'd prefer to stay here with you—sleeping or otherwise——'

'Otherwise,' decided Jassim, with a grin.

'——I've messed the Plaza around enough already. It's my duty to be on stage.'

'I understand. I agree. You do realise you owe the Indians?' he asked, as she swung herself out of bed.

'Yes. They've been very obliging, jumping in whenever I jumped out.'

'I didn't meant that. I meant if I hadn't seen them arriving at the Plaza, I'd never have chased after you and Khalid.'

Clemence paused in pulling her yellow tee-shirt over her head. 'You wouldn't?'

'No. If you remember, I'd called in as usual that evening to check that you were in place.'

'You checked to see I hadn't run off with Khalid, or vice versa,' she defined.

He moved a hand in an ineffectual gesture of agreement. 'As I was setting off down the drive for home, I met a truck heading towards the hotel. Sitting in the back were a group of Indians holding sitars, guitars, and God knows what. Nothing registered at the time and didn't do until I'd gone a good twenty miles, then——' he slapped his chest '—wham! it hit me. Why were musicians required if you were there? I turned round and went straight back. You'd vanished and so had Khalid. I grabbed hold of everyone I could and put them through the third degree. I hit lucky when the doorman reported seeing the pair of you climbing into Khalid's car. He'd overheard a mention of driving down the coast. I remembered the bay—and Ingrid—and set off.'

'In the belief that I'd gone with some devious trick in mind?' Clemence enquired, zipping up her trousers.

'I wasn't sure. At that point I wasn't too sure of anything. He realised she was almost dressed while he was still naked and leapt out of bed to begin throwing on his clothes. 'Speaking with you had almost convinced me you were straight, but logic said remember Ingrid.'

'Some logic!'

'We all make mistakes,' he said, and grabbed her and kissed her. 'And me allowing you to leave my bed just now was a big one.'

'I know,' she sighed.

Jassim held her close. 'Suppose from now on I collect you after your second show and bring you back here? Starting tonight.'

Clemence shook her head ruefully. 'After my second show tonight I have to go to the airport. I promised Howard I would. He seemed to expect me to be there to greet the wanderer returned.'

'*We'll* go to the airpot. OK? We'll collect your cousin, take him back to the hotel, settle him in, and come on here. And if you intend to accuse me of making you toe my line——'

'I don't.'

'——it's what's happening, whatever you say.'

The arrivals hall was hot, airless and crowded. Standing on tiptoe, Clemence, watched one luggage-laden passenger after another stagger out through the swing doors which led from the Customs area, but it was Jassim who recognised her cousin.

'Here comes the bridegroom,' he announced, when a figure in a voluminous beige raincoat set down two suitcases and a collection of plastic bags to look around him.

'Whatever's he wearing?' she giggled, and waved.

Howard picked up his belongings, and pushed his way through to join them. He kissed her cheek, then smiled warily at her companion.

'You've already met Jass,' she said, performing introductions.

'I have,' her cousin agreed, patently ill at ease.

Jassim grinned. 'Don't worry, Clemence has told me everything.'

'Everything?'

'Everything.' He held out his hand. 'Many congratulations on your marriage.'

Howard laughed. 'Thanks,' he said, and from then on the mood was relaxed.

'Why are you wearing that raincoat?' Clemence enquired, as the two men loaded the luggage in the boot of the BMW.

'It's a Burberry.' Her cousin reverently removed it from his shoulders. 'Do you like it?'

'Love it, but it's not exactly tropical kit, is it?'

'No, but Yvonne bought the coat for me. Sort of a wedding-present. She was keen that I wear it to Heathrow, and then although I explained how Oman was hot and dry the little love wanted me to bring the coat along as a memento of her. She became quite upset at the idea of my leaving it behind, and I didn't like to hurt her feelings, and—you know how it is?'

'Oh, I do,' Clemence assured him, while Jassim battled to keep his face straight.

Having laid the Burberry to rest with his other belongings, her cousin climbed into the back of the car.

'I've brought some wedding-cake and photographs,' he said, as they threaded their way out to the main road. 'There's so much to tell you.'

Wasting no time, Howard started his tale. For the entire journey back to the hotel, he talked non-stop; about the wedding, about the music shop, about Yvonne's star quality. His chatter was incessant and complete in itself, which was just as well, because Clemence and Jassim had become involved in a private game, the kind of game lovers play. It consisted of sidelong smiles and glances, the squeeze of a knee, a raise of a brow, and looks which throbbed with meaning. When, at last, Howard needed a reply, neither of them had heard what he'd said for ages.

'What have you been up to over the past month, Clem?' he enquired diffidently, when they drew to a halt outside the hotel. 'Been keeping busy?'

There was a long pause as she blinked herself out of the private world she shared with Jassim and into the one which included other people.

'I've tried.'

'Done anything exciting?'

A strong, tanned hand covered hers, and she smiled. 'There've been one or two moments which classify as earth-shattering.'

Her cousin sat forward. 'Oh yes?'

Jassim grinned, the dimple grooving his cheek. 'Yes. And there's a possibility the future might hold one or two more. What do you think, sunshine?'

'I think,' she said, 'you could be right.'

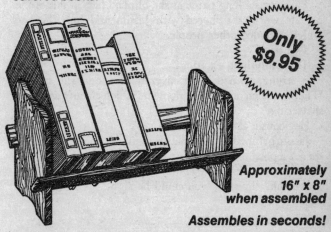

CAROLE MORTIMER

JUST ONE NIGHT

Hawk Sinclair—Texas millionaire and owner of the exclusive
Sinclair hotels, determined to protect his son's inheritance.
Leonie Spencer—desperate to protect her sister's happiness.

They were together for just one night.
The night their daughter was conceived.

Blackmail, kidnapping and attempted murder add suspense
to passion in this exciting bestseller.

The success story of Carole Mortimer continues with *Just
One Night*, a captivating romance from the author of the
bestselling novels, *Gypsy* and *Merlyn's Magic*.

**Available in March
wherever paperbacks are sold.**

Harlequin Presents

Coming Next Month

1079   DARK DESIRING   Jacqui Baird
Believing her trip to Sicily with her boss is for business, Helen finds herself trapped. Carlo Manzitti, the Italian who captured Helen's heart two years before, and from whom she had fled, has arranged the whole thing. This time he intends to keep her.

1080   THE POSITIVE APPROACH   Emma Darcy
Ben arrives in Sarah's life like a rescuing knight, with a solution to both their problems. He needs a wife; Sarah needs a fresh start. He says he'll make all her dreams come true—but eventually Sarah begins to want more than just dreams....

1081   ECHO OF PASSION   Charlotte Lamb
Zoe, hurt by Rory Ormond before, is determined to prevent the same thing happening to another young girl. She believes she's over their affair and strong enough to thwart Rory's plans without danger to her own emotions. Until she meets Rory again.

1082   LOVESCENES   Sandra Marton
Shannon angrily voices her opinion on music celebrities who walk into jobs for which real actors would give their eye teeth. Unfortunately, Cade Morgan hears her—and can't resist the challenge. That's how it all starts....

1083   WISH FOR THE MOON   Carole Mortimer
Lise Morrison was an innocent trusting girl until her love for Quinn Taylor shattered her world. But Elizabeth Farnham is less vulnerable, now, more sophisticated. She can cope with anything...except perhaps the reappearance of Quinn.

1084   TIME OUT OF MIND   Kay Thorpe
Adria Morris, suffering from amnesia, is startled when Kyle Hamilton appears and proves she is his late brother's wife. Even after her return to their family home on St. Amelia, her amnesia persists. Adria must decide whether to marry Kyle, or leave behind all hope of regaining her memory.

1085   LOST LAGOON   Anne Weale
Interior designer Alexandra, headed for the top, isn't going to be swayed from her career, even by someone as special as Laurier Tait. And Laurier isn't the type to settle for a brief autumn affair—he wants a full-time partner in life.

1086   THE ORTIGA MARRIAGE   Patricia Wilson
Meriel has made a life of her own since her stepbrother, Ramon Ortiga, rejected her love. Now, because of her young half brother, Manuel, she returns to the remote Venezuelan ranch to find Ramon as arrogant as ever—and her attraction to him still as strong.

Available in June wherever paperback books are sold, or through Harlequin Reader Service:

In the U.S.
901 Fuhrmann Blvd.
P.O. Box 1397
Buffalo, N.Y. 14240-1397

In Canada
P.O. Box 603
Fort Erie, Ontario
L2A 5X3

Penny Jordan

Stronger than Yearning

He was the man of her dreams!

The same dark hair, the same mocking eyes; it was as if the Regency rake of the portrait, the seducer of Jenna's dream, had come to life. Jenna, believing the last of the Deverils dead, was determined to buy the great old Yorkshire Hall—to claim it for her daughter, Lucy, and put to rest some of the painful memories of Lucy's birth. She had no way of knowing that a direct descendant of the black sheep Deveril even existed—or that James Allingham and his own powerful yearnings would disrupt her plan entirely.

Penny Jordan's first Harlequin Signature Edition *Love's Choices* was an outstanding success. Penny Jordan has written more than 40 best-selling titles—more than 4 million copies sold.

Now, be sure to buy her latest bestseller, *Stronger Than Yearning*. Available wherever paperbacks are sold—in June.

STRONG-1R